STORM WATCHER

New York Times Bestselling Author

Maria V. Snyder

Storm Watcher

COPYRIGHT© 2013 by Maria V. Snyder

Contact Information: leapbks@gmail.com

Cover Art by *Ahyoung Moon*

Sketches by *Maria V. Snyder* pgs. 186-7, 195-6, 198, 203, 206, 218-9; all other graphics by Leap Books

Leap Books
Powell, WY
www.leapbks.net
Publishing History
First Leap Edition 2013
ISBN: 978-1-61603-033-9

Library of Congress Control Number: 2013950448

Published in the United States of America

Praise for *New York Times* Bestselling
Author Maria V. Snyder's

STORM WATCHER

"Best selling author Maria V. Snyder's debut novel for young readers, STORM WATCHER, is a thrilling, heart-warming canine caper. Thirteen-year-old Luke loves dogs and is fascinated with weather data—but storms terrify him. With lightning-quick action, humor, and lots of dogs, STORM WATCHER will delight young readers. Also the scientific and math insights into weather will appeal to educators and inspire readers to create their own weather science projects. Highly recommended!"

~ **Linda Joy Singleton**, *author of THE SEER and DEAD GIRL series*

"Snyder's lightning strikes again with STORM WATCH-ER's tale of ordinary people fighting to become heroes in the face of things they fear most. Luke's story is by turns funny, touching, and achingly real, as Snyder harnesses a lifetime of expertise about meteorology, dogs, and life in small towns."

~ **Morgan Keyes**, *author of the DARKBEAST series*

"STORM WATCHER is a brilliant and beautiful tale of how the simple, honest love of a dog can help a lonely boy find his way out of the darkness. Subtle, powerful and highly recommended."

~ **Jonathan Maberry**, *New York Times Bestselling author of FIRE & ASH and ROT & RUIN*

Also by Maria V. Snyder

Acknowledgments

Where to start? I guess I should go way back and thank the lady who hired me to work in her kennel a long time ago during the summer between graduating college and working as a meteorologist. Is it terrible that I can't remember her name, but I can remember all the dogs' names? I love dogs and working with more than fifty of them was the *best* job, aside from writing, that I ever had. Plus the experience eventually led to this book.

I also want to thank my writing critique group that helped me with this story. Without the guidance and encouragement from the York Muse and Schmooze critique group when I was a member, I wouldn't be a published author today. Thanks so much, Shawn, Laurie, Julie, Lisa, Anne, Steve, Maggie, Lori, Kim, Jackie, Mike, and Nancy. I miss you guys!

Special thanks to Kat O'Shea for all her hard work (and then some) in getting this story in tip-top shape! And thanks to Ahyoung Moon for the perfect cover.

A big thank you goes to my family. To my husband, Rodney for all the support and for bragging about me to everyone he meets. Thanks to my daughter, Jenna, for her feedback on teen speak and inspiration – Sumo Kitty is for you. And a huge thank you to my Luke. His humor and wit not only make me laugh, but inspire me to add humor to my stories.

Dedication

This one is for Luke, my goofy son who is not the Luke in the story because my Luke likes cats (I blame his father) and is proud to be the annoying older brother.

In memory of Julie Good, a talented writer and exceptional woman, who was instrumental in my success. Thank you for everything, Julie. You won't be forgotten.

CHAPTER 1

Mutant Fur Ball

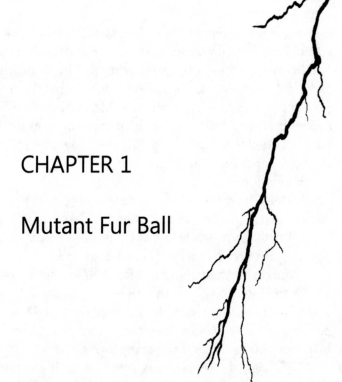

Everything changed the day Luke's mom died. No surprise, right? Of course things changed. He'd be stupid to expect anything else. But what surprised him the most was what *hadn't* changed.

Luke hovered on the edge of the American Kennel Club's tracking event, invisible to all but a few. People and dogs milled about, waiting for their turn to run the course and follow scent trails laid in a large grassy field. Barks, yips, and growls mixed with the buzz of voices and the louder calls of handlers encouraging their pets to stay on the trail and earn their tracking certificates.

Luke had been to dozens of these events, and

nothing was different about today's show. Actually since school ended five days ago, he should be ecstatic. But the familiar noise of the AKC event drummed in his hollow chest. He wanted to scream at everyone. To tell them to stop and realize a person was missing. A woman who had embarrassed him with her loud cheering, unwanted advice, and sideline coaching as if she knew more than the dog's handlers – she didn't.

He couldn't.

Instead, he listened to his older twin brothers act all big and bad – another thing that hadn't changed.

"What's that white speck?" Jacob asked Scott, pointing at a group of handlers and dogs.

"Mutant fur ball come to life. Coughed up by our very own Hounddog. Isn't that right, Hounddog?" Scott leaned over and rubbed the long ears of the bloodhound panting at his feet. "You stay away from that little fur ball, Hounddog. That's no squeaky toy."

Luke sighed. His brothers acted so cool, but their non-stop chatter meant they were nervous. This was the first time their dogs, Hounddog and Moondoggie, would run an official AKC course.

"Hey, isn't that one of those papillons?" Scott asked Luke.

Squinting into the bright sunlight, Luke studied the mutant fur ball in question. Small with white long hair, black ears, and black patches around her eyes, she stood out amid the beefy German shepherds, bloodhounds, and retrievers, who waited for their turn to sniff the trail.

"Yeah," Luke said. "Except it's pronounced *pappy-yawn*." He didn't add the name meant *butterfly* in French. It'd result in instant teasing from the twins.

"*That's* the dog you want for your birthday?" Jacob

asked with a laugh. "It'd be either squished or eaten by one of our bloods as soon as you brought it home."

"Papillons are good trackers," Luke said in the dog's defense.

"No way Dad will agree," Scott added. "You'd better stick to a bloodhound."

But the thought of owning a bloodhound failed to excite Luke. They already owned three. And when Luke and Mom had researched the various dog breeds last year, they'd discovered the petite papillon.

The breed had all the qualities of a bloodhound, but in a small, powerful package. And the idea of owning one appealed to him. Maybe because a papillon looked like the exact opposite of a bloodhound. Maybe because his brothers had accused him of being a copycat since… forever. Maybe because his Mom had loved the idea.

"This dog is just what you're looking for." Mom had tapped the computer screen with excitement. "Papillons are friendly, intelligent, tough, and have a strong instinct to protect. Just like you."

"Me?"

"Yes, you. Remember when you were four and Alicia Weber was picking on Scott and you jumped between them and chased her off?" Mom laughed.

Luke didn't, but this was one of Mom's favorite stories.

"You were half her size, but, boy, she was scared of you. The papillon might be small, but I'd bet she'd stand up to the bloodhounds."

"She?"

"It'd be nice to have another female around the house," Mom joked.

Luke spun a pencil around, both thrilled and

nervous about the idea. "Dad wouldn't like it."

"Then you'll just have to convince him," Mom had said as if that was the easiest thing in the world to do.

It wasn't. Luke's stomach twisted. Dad wouldn't talk about it even though Luke's thirteenth birthday was only a week away.

Luke scanned the crowd, searching for his dad. Shaking hands, chatting, and smiling, Dad weaved his way through the press of people like a bloodhound on a fresh trail. As the only electrician in town, he knew everyone.

Eventually Dad joined them. "Boys, pay attention to the Tracking Dog Test. You'll learn a lot about how to handle a dog." Dad said to Luke, "After the event's over, go and talk to Mr. Johnson. Any of his pups would make a nice addition to our little kennel." Dad's gaze slid back to the crowd, and he hurried off without waiting for a response.

Scott chewed his lip. Jacob knotted Moondoggie's leash in his hands. Luke'd been right. They were scared about running their dogs.

Jacob noticed Luke staring at him. "Whatcha lookin' at, Weather Weenie? Go watch the clouds. I think I saw a little baby thunderstorm heading this way."

"Better go hide, Lukie," Scott said.

Anger boiled inside, but Luke clamped his mouth shut before he said something that would start a fight. Bigger, stronger, and smellier, his older brothers always ganged up on him and wrestled him to the ground until he gave in. *Not fair.*

A gust of wind touched his sweaty brow. Luke glanced up. A few dark clouds stained the sky. Fear churned in his guts.

Calm down. Deep breath, Luke repeated.

Memories from another storm flashed in his mind. His body numbed, and icy steel jaws bit deep into his soul as the image of his mother floated in front of him. Pain, bitter and unrelenting, pulsed in his chest as he thought for the thousandth time: *I shouldn't have called. It's all my fault.*

With a hard lump in his throat, Luke struggled to keep from curling into a ball. A sympathetic nose pressed against his knee. He glanced down into Moondoggie's warm brown eyes. Bending to give Jacob's hound a hug, Luke didn't care what his brothers thought. Just the feel of a soft chin on his shoulder, and the musky smell of dog helped ease the tightness in his chest.

Scott said, "Look at that mangy lot. Ranger'll be the only dog to get a Tracking Dog title today."

"No kidding. Dad and Ranger are a *professional* Search and Rescue team." Jacob said loudly. He scanned the crowd as if hoping people around them were close enough to hear his boast.

Luke stood. *Here we go again.*

Scott joined in. "Yeah, Dad was *specifically* requested to go to Colorado to find those lost climbers. SAR is one of his jobs, these others are just..."

"Hobbyists," Jacob said, snorting with disdain.

That's it. Sick of their obnoxiousness, Luke walked over to find a good spot to watch the TD event. A dog had to show an impressive amount of skill to earn a TD title. The tracks had been made at least thirty minutes ago. And some were two hours old. Despite the strong odor of fresh cut grass, the dogs smelled human scent on the ground and followed it.

A few dogs lost the scent, and the cheers from the

crowd distracted others. When Ranger approached the starting line, Luke scrunched the bottom of his shirt as his heart raced. He might be tired of bloodhounds, but Luke had grown up with Ranger.

Nose to the ground and ears dragging, Ranger found the first turn. It was to the left, so the next one would be a right. Luke held his breath as Dad encouraged Ranger. And just when he thought Ranger had missed it, the bloodhound made a sharp right.

The half turn would be the hardest. Luke rose onto his tiptoes to see better. Ranger paused.

Come on.

The dog lifted his head and glanced at the crowd.

Oh no.

Then Ranger resumed snuffling. Breaking into a trot, he jigged to the right and scooped up the glove in his mouth.

Show off. Luke cheered with the rest of the onlookers. Dad beamed.

But it didn't take long for the well wishers to disperse. A growing murmur of excitement and surprise drew them to another scent trail. In a blur of white, the "mutant fur ball" dog zipped along the track and found the glove without hesitation. Applause exploded.

Even Dad appeared impressed. Luke's hopes rose. If Dad knew that dog was a papillon, maybe he wouldn't be so dead set against Luke getting one for his birthday.

Excitement built when Luke spotted Dad talking to the handler of the white dog after the AKC event. She was as tall as Dad, with gray-streaked black hair braided down her back.

Luke sidled over to his father. They didn't notice him, but the petite dog danced over, tail wagging. Luke knelt on the ground, letting her sniff his hand.

"Hey, girl," he said as he scratched her head.

Her black ears perked up at the sound of his voice. She had the most unusually shaped ears he'd ever seen. Each side looked like half of a butterfly.

She was the perfect size. Small enough to take anywhere. And she wouldn't hog the bed. After all, Dad had broken his own rule about no dogs in the house, letting Ranger sleep in the empty space next to him on the bed. And the twins had each other. They never needed their dogs for companionship. So Luke was sure he could convince Dad once his new puppy was housebroken.

This dog had the perfect temperament. Happy and curious. She snuffled at his pockets, then put her front paws on his legs, reaching to lick his chin. And she stared at him as if he were the only person in the world.

She was smart, too. Luke pretended to throw a rock, but she didn't fall for that trick. She watched for the rock to leave his hand before racing after it.

Luke grinned at the thought of having a puppy like her waiting for him at home, being excited to see him, and sharing a room with him. Would Dad agree? Luke's enthusiasm died. Probably not.

"She likes you," the woman said.

Luke glanced up into the iron gray eyes of the handler. Dad had disappeared. *Figures.* Flustered, Luke sat there with his mouth open.

"Are you one of Jim Riley's boys?" she asked.

He nodded, and cleared his throat. "Luke Riley, ma'am."

"Willajean. I hear you're looking for a pup. I have some bloodhounds that'll be ready by the end of July.

Interested?"

"No." Surprised by his boldness, Luke couldn't stop the flow of words from his mouth. "I'm actually interested in a papillon."

Willajean cocked her head, sizing Luke up. "I see."

Luke stood and brushed the dirt off his knees. "Are papillons hard to train?"

"Nope. Hardy little dogs, not princesses like some of those other toy breeds. I'm waiting for Sweetie's sister to whelp any day now. That litter'll be ready by the end of August."

Upon hearing her name, the white dog yipped. Willajean picked her up. They looked like opposites. Soft and billowy next to hard and lean.

Dad reappeared. "Luke, great news. Mr. Johnson said you could have your pick of the litter."

Luke stammered and cringed. The broad smile on Dad's face wavered. Willajean, expressionless, turned away. But Luke needed her. If he were to tell Dad what he really wanted, she had to be there so his dad wouldn't ignore him. Plus if she left, he would lose his nerve and wind up with a bloodhound pup.

"Wait, please?" he asked Willajean.

She stopped.

"Dad, you know I love bloodhounds, but I've been thinking we should branch out and try another breed."

"Which breed?" Dad asked in a monotone.

Luke recognized that tone. It meant Dad was mad. Luke gathered his courage. *Now or never.* "A papillon."

Confusion and surprise warred on Dad's face. "I'm all for considering a different breed, but a papillon is – ah, no offense, Willajean – useless for search and rescue. It's one thing to find a glove in an open field, but she'd never be able to keep up in the thick underbrush of the woods."

"But I'm not doing search and rescue. I thought the puppy would be mine." Luke's voice cracked, and he flushed with embarrassment.

"No, Luke. No papillon. You pick a bloodhound pup. Or no pup."

CHAPTER 2

Pooper Scooper

Luke gaped at Dad as a tight band of pressure ringed his chest. Disappointment turned into anger, but Dad's hard stare dared him to talk back. A gust of wind rustled Dad's shirt.

Luke swallowed an outraged protest. "Fine." The word slipped out between tight lips. "I'll get a blood-hound, but I want one of Ms..."

"Willajean," she said curtly.

"I want one of Willajean's pups." Luke held his breath, waiting for Dad's reply. If he had to resign himself to a bloodhound, he wasn't about to give in all the way and get the one Dad wanted.

Dad ran a hand through thick black hair beginning

to gray. His tanned and well-muscled forearms stood out against his white polo shirt. In a flat tone, he said, "Ben Johnson owes me a dog in lieu of stud fees. Even though Willajean is new to this area, her excellent reputation has preceded her, and with such exceptional bloodlines, I'm sure I won't be able to afford one of her pups."

Luke's shoulders sagged. He'd forgotten how expensive a well-bred pup was. Dad had made them painfully aware of their financial situation after Mom died. He had sat down with them and explained how much they'd relied on Mom's salary and health benefits. Then on Jacob and Scott's sixteenth birthday last month, instead of having a big party, they'd started working at Hersheypark.

"That's no problem." Willajean's authoritative voice pierced Luke's gloom. "Luke can work in my kennel this summer, and as payment he can have his pick of the litter." When Dad protested, Willajean interrupted. "You live on Longshore Avenue, right? I see your electrician's truck at night when I go to the grocery store."

Dad nodded.

"Your house is within biking distance of my farm. I only need help a few days a week, and Luke'll learn how to handle a dog for tracking and for show."

Who could argue with that? Hope surged in Luke's heart. As his father mulled over the offer, Willajean winked at Luke. She seemed determined to help him, but he wasn't sure why. Good breeders usually had a long waiting list of buyers.

"A generous proposal," Dad finally admitted. He searched Luke's face. "This is a serious commitment. Make *sure* this is what you want before accepting Willajean's offer."

For Dad's benefit, Luke paused. But as soon as Willajean had offered to employ him, he wanted it more than anything else. Their house was too quiet, too empty, and contained too many reminders of Mom. He'd rather work than be home alone all day watching the Weather Channel.

"Sounds great. When do I start?" Luke asked.

"Monday morning. Seven o'clock."

Ugh. Dad smirked. Luke and mornings didn't get along.

Despite the early time, Luke's excitement didn't die. He had something to do this summer. He shook Willajean's hand. "See you at seven."

"Come on, Pooper Scooper. Time to get up," Scott cried with vicious delight as he yanked the sheet off Luke the next morning. Scott's laughter echoed in the hallway as he thumped down the steps.

Luke groaned and rolled over. He blinked, focusing on the clock. Six fifteen.

Like a fly caught in a sticky cobweb, he struggled to get out of his comfortable bed. Finally winning the battle, he schlepped to the bathroom. Bleary eyed, Luke dressed in old clothes and joined his brothers and father in the kitchen.

Jacob and Scott had been loud and obnoxious ever since their dogs had earned a Tracking Instinct certificate. As he ate his cold cereal, Luke had to listen for the millionth time about how Hounddog and Moondoggie ruled while Dad read the newspaper and ignored them.

Unlike Luke, his brothers had energy in the morning. They woke early every day for swim team practice before reporting to work. Luke shivered just thinking about jumping into a pool of water before noon.

"Better get moving, Pooper Scooper," Jacob said. "You don't want to be late on your first day. There're steaming piles just waiting for you to clean up."

Here we go. Luke kept his gaze on his bowl, knowing the smartest thing to do was to ignore Jacob. Mom would have stopped the teasing right away, but since March the twins had been hammering on him at any opportunity. And for them, anything he said or did was an opportunity.

"Some advice for the working boy – hold the pan steady and move the poop into the pan with the scraper, instead of trying to scoop it up with the pan." Scott teased. "It's a bone-a-fide technique that'll get you promoted to dog bather within weeks."

"You should know, Scottie," Luke countered, rising to the bait. "Based on the amount of time you spend in the bathroom, I would say you're an expert in poop management."

Scott drew breath to reply, but Dad interrupted with a stern, "That's enough, boys."

Finally.

As Luke biked to Willajean's farm, he thought about his brothers. He hated arguing with them, but lately they never gave him a break. They teased him about watching the Weather Channel all the time, about having no friends – not like Luke could change that, his best friend had gotten really weird after Mom died and stopped hanging out with him. Jacob and Scott treated him like he was a scab that needed to be picked.

Apprehension tugged his guts when his suburban neighborhood turned into wide fields of soybeans, corn, and tobacco. Willajean's entrance was between two fenced fields. *Storm Watcher Kennel* was etched in gold on a wooden sign at the top of the gravel driveway. Luke skidded to a stop. He reread the kennel's name. A practical joke? He expected his brothers to jump out from behind the sign and yell *gotcha*.

Luke scanned the skies, seeking ominous clouds despite the Weather Channel's forecast that a high-pressure system would dominate the region, causing an uneventful, sunny day. Sometimes the Weather Channel was wrong, but not usually for the short-term forecast. And Luke had watched for a full hour last night just to be sure.

Satisfied that no dark clouds threatened, Luke coasted down the long driveway. Small corn plants grew in neat rows on the left side, and a pasture of cows grazed on the right. At the bottom several buildings, an old two-story barn, and a massive stone house sat on a grassy hill.

Deep barks, woofs, and high-pitched yips all emanated from a long, thin structure with wire-fenced kennel runs behind it. Parking his bike against the wall, Luke opened the screen door and entered a kitchen. He stopped short. The sound of sizzling meat mixed with the aroma of hamburgers. Amazed to find a kitchen inside a dog kennel, he gazed at the refrigerator, freezer, microwave, stove, dishwasher, and a sink.

Willajean stood next to the stove. She dumped a pan full of cooked ground beef into a huge mixing bowl held by a young girl with short brown hair.

"Good. You're just in time." Willajean wiped her

hands on her apron.

Luke gawked when Willajean and the girl added ground eggshells, cooked eggs, carrot slices, chopped onions, cooked rice, oatmeal, vinegar, oil, and some funky-looking fatty globs into the bowl. His stomach flip-flopped between craving the delicious-smelling mixture and being nauseated by it.

Once Willajean combined the assortment, she spooned portions into metal bowls that were weighed on a scale.

"Roulette," she said, handing the bowl to the girl. After stuffing various pills deep into the food, the girl hurried around the corner.

"The Emperor," she ordered, thrusting the next bowl at Luke. At his confused expression she said, "Put one vitamin from each pile into the food, then follow Megan. The dogs' names are on their doors."

Luke mashed the pills into the food and ran after Megan. Turning the corner, he almost tripped over his own feet. The room was longer than his house. Along the left wall, metal crates were stacked two high with one dog inside each. On the right, doors led out to the kennel runs.

The dogs' barking intensified as he slowly moved down the row, reading names and counting – thirty dogs in all. Willajean owned and bred bloodhounds, papillons, and German shepherds. *Wow*. Luke was impressed and a little jealous. Near the end of the row, he found the crate marked *Emperor*. A papillon peered at him through the bars, then stepped back, giving Luke room to put the bowl down.

True to his name, Emperor took small bites and regarded Luke with regal distain. The complete opposite of Hounddog, who devoured his dry generic food in seconds.

"Luke, hurry up," Willajean called.

He raced back to the kitchen, and soon the ordered chaos of feeding time consumed him. Bowl after bowl went to dogs named, Jackson, Ike, Sarah, Libby, Black Jack, Shasta, Maggie, Tanner, Hazel. All the names blended together, and Luke puffed with the effort of delivering food. His brothers would never believe him about the number of dogs or the incredible food – not what he'd imagined his first day would be like at all.

After breakfast, the dogs were let out of their crates and guided to their runs to do their business. Once finished they were taken to fenced fields. Luke leaned on the gate. The dogs chased each other with boundless energy.

"Luke, this is my daughter, Megan," Willajean said, hooking her thumb at the girl.

A couple inches taller than Luke, Megan had dark brown eyes with thick eyebrows. She wore a stained yellow T-shirt, cut-off jeans, and boots. Crossing her arms, she studied him. He wondered if she was angry that her mom hired him.

"She's going to your school this September, starting eighth grade. Same as you, right?"

"Yeah," he said.

Megan shot her mom a look. Luke wasn't sure what it meant, but Willajean ignored it.

"Megan, clean up the runs, show Luke around, and then take Bonnie and Clyde over to the tracking course," Willajean instructed. With a wave, she strode toward the house.

Megan handed Luke a metal pan and scraper. Ugh.

He crinkled his nose, thinking about Scott's unwelcome advice that morning.

She laughed. "Better get used to it. We clean up twice a day." Megan opened the closest run. She picked up a pile with one quick stroke of the scraper, then moved on. "Besides, it's way better than changing diapers."

"What?" Luke fumbled at the catch on the next run.

"My older sister." Now it was Megan's turn to make an *ugh* face. "Babysitter extraordinaire. The reason Mom needed extra help. Alayna would rather wipe noses and butts, and deal with whiny ankle biters all day than work here." Megan emptied her pan into a bucket. "I'll take being with dogs over kids any time."

They worked in silence until the runs were clean.

"Now comes the fun part." Megan leaned over one of the gates and yelled for Bonnie and Clyde.

Luke glanced around. Written onto the gate for each field were the names of the dogs that went into that field.

"Why four separate fields? And what's with the names everywhere?" he asked. They were on the runs, too.

"Mom's paranoid. Some dogs don't get along. If you put them in a run or field together, they'll fight." Megan shrugged. "Fact of life. Back in North Carolina, Mom lost her favorite German shepherd when he was accidentally placed in the wrong run."

Wow. A dog died. How could she be so…uncaring?

She noticed him staring. "We're breeders. We can't get attached to the dogs, or this place would be overflowing with dogs, and we'd have no money to pay for food."

Luke considered. It made sense. Maybe hanging out with Megan would help him develop a similar tough attitude.

Megan called for the dogs again, this time louder.

"Why don't you let the dogs do their business in the fields?" he asked. "Then we wouldn't have to clean it up."

Megan gave him an incredulous look. "Do you even own a dog?"

"We have three," he said in his defense.

"Oh that's not enough. I've been around dogs all my life, and you can't let dogs poop anywhere. Some like to roll in it, and others like to eat it. It's really gross."

Ugh. He lost his appetite. Soon two black-and-tan bloodhounds came loping into sight, tongues lolling, tails wagging. Megan let them out. They pranced around her, and she lavished hugs on them. Then the dogs followed behind Luke and Megan as they walked to the training yard.

Glancing at his watch, Luke couldn't believe it was nine o'clock already. A grassy field with small orange cones and an old shed marked the training area. Willajean stood nearby, tapping on her tablet computer.

Before they entered, Megan said, "Don't step past the cones. Mom's already laid the tracks for the dogs to practice. See?"

Luke squinted into the sunlight. The cones marked where Willajean had made a series of scent trails. Easy enough to do. Leave a scent article at the beginning – most people used gloves. Walk on the grass for at least fifty yards, make one left or right turn, go straight, make another turn in the opposite direction, go straight, make a half turn, go straight, and then drop a glove with your scent on it at the end. The entire trail must be at least 440 yards long, with each leg at least 50 yards long. The more experienced dogs ran over courses with more turns.

Willajean tested the dogs in pairs. Bonnie and Clyde sailed through without trouble. Megan rewarded them with a game of Frisbee before sending them back to their field with Luke. He called for Jackson and Ike, and they repeated the training.

Entering information about each dog into her tablet, Willajean said, "I have so many dogs, and they're all at different levels of training. This" – she waved the tablet – "has been a big time saver."

Being the rookie, Luke was given the easiest tasks. Fetching harnesses and leads, escorting dogs, and cleaning up accidents.

They stopped for a quick lunch break. Luke's appetite returned full force, and he wished he remembered to bring food. When Megan and Willajean went inside, he sat next to his bike. At least he hadn't forgotten to fill his water bottle. He chugged the lukewarm water. *Yuck*.

After lunch they continued the training. Hot and sweaty, Luke dragged his feet, wishing for a candy bar, or rather a box of candy bars.

Finally, Willajean called, "That's everyone. Luke, go help Megan feed the puppies and set up for tomorrow. Then you can go home. I'll need you on Mondays, Wednesdays, and Fridays. Is that okay with your schedule?"

Since watching the Weather Channel was the only thing on his schedule this summer, he nodded, glad she hadn't changed her mind about their arrangement. He'd worked harder today than…well, ever.

"Great, see you then." Willajean headed to the house.

Luke followed Megan back to the kennel.

Megan pulled out frozen white squares from the freezer and handed them to Luke.

"Put these on the counter," she said.

The words, *liver*, *tripe*, and *beef* had been written on them. Luke set them down. "Tripe?"

"Cow's stomach."

Eww. "What're these for?"

"Dog food." Megan gave him a cutting board and knife and set him chopping onions and carrots while she cooked rice.

"Oh. These dogs eat better than me," Luke said. "Your parents must be rich."

Megan had finished chopping and now weighed bowls of food. She shrugged. "Mom inherited this farm from Poppy, her dad, this year. We moved here in April. Thank goodness my father had already run off, or he would've ruined everything."

A fierce frown gripped Megan's face for an instant. She shook her head as if to push her father from her mind. "Although Poppy's probably giving everyone grief in heaven, griping that my mother turned a perfectly good Black Angus cattle ranch into a kennel."

"Black Angus? Really?"

She laughed. "Yep. And just to make him madder, she's feeding the dogs his prize-winning Black Angus steers. One at a time."

CHAPTER 3

The Peck-and-Run Maneuver

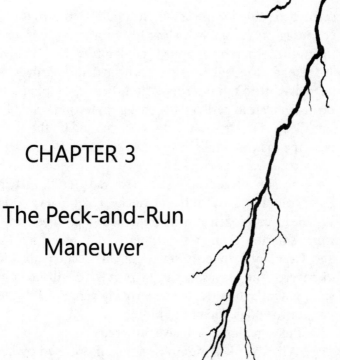

Bored, Luke prowled around the house the next morning. He'd already walked both Hounddog and Moondoggie, watched two hours of the Weather Channel, and cleaned out his backpack. Finally, he jumped on his bike and pedaled to Storm Watcher Kennel. Willajean and Megan ran a chubby German shepherd named Tanner through a scent trail in the training yard.

With hardly a hello, Willajean sent Luke to fetch dogs. Before he left, Megan raised her eyebrows at him. Probably wondering why he was here, but Luke just shrugged, not sure either.

He spent the rest of the afternoon laying tracks through the cornfield for the dogs to follow. He placed scent pads filled with small treats along the route to encourage the dogs to follow his scent from one pad to another. Then he wrapped the dog treat in the glove at the end. The leaves of the corn tickled his calves as he walked through the rows, careful not to step on any plants. Willajean had said the change in terrain would be a challenge for a few of the dogs. Tracks laid on the grass were the easiest to follow, then parking lots. Woods and city streets were the hardest.

The sun blazed and sweat soaked his T-shirt as Luke completed five different tracks. Luke marveled as Willajean or Megan ran behind each dog. These dogs were smarter than his brothers. The bloodhounds and German shepherds stayed on his scent path and discovered the gloves. As an extra reward, all the dogs were praised, then treated to a rowdy game of Frisbee. Fun for the dogs, Luke, and Megan.

"Luke, get lost," Willajean ordered.

"What?" Luke's mouth hung open, stunned by her harsh words.

"Lost in the woods." She pointed to the trees surrounding the farm. "Tracks in a cornfield are okay for AKC titles, but I'm training Lance to be an air-scenting search and rescue dog."

Puzzled, Luke asked, "What's the difference?"

"A tracking dog tracks with its nose to the ground, focusing its attention on contact and ground scent. But an air-scenting dog picks up *airborne* human scent." Willajean bent over and scratched Lance behind his ears. "Once, at a demonstration, I saw a dog find a specific man in a large crowd. The dog's nose was in the air the whole time. Amazing." Willajean shook her head as if she still couldn't believe what she had witnessed.

Willajean gave Luke a white towel. He wiped his sweaty face on it and handed it back. Then he hiked through the woods for a half an hour, crunching through the dead leaves, and zigzagging past bushes before he found a great spot to hide next to a fallen tree. Dirt still clung to the roots, and its leaves were still green. Luke laid flat, breathing in the scent of wet earth. Insects buzzed overhead. How long should he wait? What if Lance didn't find him?

After a while, other sounds reached him. The shuffle of a small animal, scurrying through the underbrush. Birds flying from limb to limb, calling out to each other. A loud mockingbird perched nearby, showing off by singing all its songs. Luke counted the different calls for something to do. Thirteen. Not bad, little bird.

A distant bark silenced all the noise. Then the unmistakable tread of footsteps and jingle of dog tags. In no time, the German shepherd leapt over the tree trunk. Excited, Lance jumped on Luke, licking his face and slobbering all over him. *Eww.*

"Lance, heel," Willajean said, coming up behind the dog. "Sorry about that. He's young yet. Another six months should help him mature."

Luke had learned more about dogs during the one week he'd worked at Willajean's than he had in a lifetime living with Dad. Fascinated by Willajean's knowledge, he had turned his days off into half-days. Plus there'd been no rain and no storms. Luke almost felt – not quite normal – but better than he had since Mom died.

When they finished training on Friday afternoon,

Willajean called to Luke, "Come with me, Lost-and-Found. I want to show you something."

Luke's heart did a tight double squeeze in his chest. He hadn't been inside the house yet. And what did she mean by *lost-and-found*? Perhaps she was merely referring to his daily task of getting lost in the woods.

She led him through the house. He gawked at all the rooms they passed. One after another. This place was humongous. Boxes were stacked everywhere. But a few areas had been unpacked. A flat, wide-screen TV that had to be at least fifty-two inches hung on the wall of the living room with a brand new video game system underneath. Luke wanted to stop and drool over the tall stack of video games, but didn't.

The longest table he'd ever seen filled the dining room. It would make a great bike ramp. Stopping in an enclosed sun porch, Willajean pointed to a large wooden whelping box. Sprawled inside was a sleeping bloodhound, surprising because seven puppies roughhoused nearby.

"Here's the litter. They were born on June first, so at the end of July you can take one home – a belated birthday present."

"Uh…yeah that's great." Luke tried to get excited about his birthday tomorrow, but without Mom it just wouldn't be the same. No off-key singing. No girly-color wrapping paper. No over-cooked cake. He swallowed. How could the things that had annoyed him so much before be missed so much it hurt deep down inside? He'd actually been trying to forget about his birthday. And although the blood pups were super cute, they grew into big dogs just like the three they already had at home. Did he even want one?

"Do you have a name picked out yet?" Willajean asked.

Luke hadn't considered names. He cleared his throat. "No. But I know I'd like a female." For Mom. Plus Dad couldn't say no to that.

A papillon raced into the room, barking and yipping, obviously agitated. Willajean picked the dog up. "Well, you might want to wait until you get to know your dog. They have distinct personalities. Isn't that right, Sweetie?" Willajean asked the papillon. Sweetie squirmed, and Willajean set her down. She raced to the door, then stopped and glanced at Willajean. She whined.

"What's the matter?" Willajean followed the dog.

Luke stood in the sunroom, uncertain if he should go or stay.

After a couple minutes, Willajean came running back with a white mass in her arms and Sweetie yipping at her heels. "Lady's in labor. She's early. Luke, quick, get that white box off the shelf."

"Uh." Luke stammered, but he spotted the box and struggled to get it down.

When he placed it on the floor, Willajean pointed to a bag full of towels. "Use them to cover the bottom."

He spread them out.

Willajean laid the dog on top. "Go get Megan, please."

Luke ran to the kennel's kitchen.

"Where ya been?" Megan asked as soon as he burst into the room.

"Lady." He gasped. "In...labor."

"Already?" Megan washed her hands.

How could she be so calm? Luke wanted to rush back

to the house, but kept pace with Megan. By the time they returned, poor Lady was panting and shaking.

Pulling on a pair of latex gloves, Megan helped Lady while Luke and Willajean watched. He was unable to tear his gaze away. Lady strained, and a blob came out her back end, followed by a gush of blood. Gross. The blob didn't resemble a puppy at all. Covered with a see-through film, it had a string that went back inside Lady.

Megan moved the blob closer to Lady's head. Lady chewed off the sack, and cleaned the pup with her tongue. Really gross.

Megan pointed to a gooey mass and said, "That's the placenta, and this is the umbilical cord." She held the pup up, and Lady cut the cord with her teeth. "You gotta make sure the mother dog doesn't chew off the puppy's tail."

When the pup was clean, it squeaked and squealed.

"It's a girl." Megan guided the pup to a nipple to suck.

Then nothing happened.

"Only one?" Luke asked disappointed.

"Probably not," Willajean said. "It takes time. Do you want to help with the next one?"

Shocked, he glanced at her. "Can I? Really?"

"Of course." She smiled. "This is a natural process. Lady doesn't really need any help unless there're complications. We like to be on hand to guide the pups to feed and make sure none of them are accidently smothered under Lady or in the towels. Unfortunately, it happens." Willajean tsked. "You'll need to wash your hands and put on gloves first."

Luke ran to kitchen, scrubbed his hands and arms up to his elbows, dried them, and raced back. He didn't want to miss the next one.

"You might as well get comfortable," Megan said. "This could be awhile."

"Do you want to call your dad and let him know you'll be late?" Willajean asked.

Luke glanced at the clock – four thirty. "No, he won't be home until six or seven."

"Okay, guess I'll start dinner. Do you like mac and cheese, Luke?"

"Yeah."

"Good." Willajean left.

Ten minutes later, Lady grunted and another puppy blob slid out. Luke gently pulled the slippery and warm pup closer to Lady's head. Beyond cool. When all the yucky stuff had been licked off, he helped the pup find a nipple.

Two hours and one bowl of mac and cheese later, Lady finished giving birth. She had three females and two males in the litter. Willajean praised Lady.

"Wow," Luke said. "That was the coolest thing I ever saw." He grinned, but his smile dimmed. In eight weeks all the puppies would be sold, and Lady would be without her babies. And just as bad, the babies would be without their mother. Just like him.

"It's a shame you can't keep all the puppies," Luke said.

"I already have too many dogs." Seeming to sense his mood, Willajean added, "Once the puppies are weaned, they no longer need their mothers. They're different than us. Besides I couldn't think of that many names."

"You said that papillons are tough dogs. But you have one dog called Sweetie and another called Lady. How come?"

"Well, Lady's real name is Painted Lady, which is a species of butterfly. Sweetie's real name is Mourning Cloak, another species, but she's the sweetest dog I've ever owned, so no other nickname would stick." Willajean shrugged. "I was trying to be clever by naming my papillons after butterfly species, but some of the names tanked, like Swallow Tail, and I get strange looks at the AKC events."

"Does that bother you?" Luke thought about how much effort his brothers put into naming their dogs, hoping to sound way cool.

"No. Actually if I don't get at least one odd look a day, I start wondering what's the matter." She laughed at Luke's expression. "See, now I'm all set for tonight. Megan will be happy. I don't have to embarrass her at the mall."

"Not like it ever stopped you before," Megan teased.

A wave of sorrow swept over Luke. He'd teased Mom about always embarrassing him at Jacob and Scott's swim meets. She'd stand on the bleachers and cheer at the top of her lungs.

"I have to be loud," she'd say. "So the boys can hear me through the water."

On his bike ride home, Luke thought about Willajean. She was straightforward, almost blunt. Plus she treated him like an adult and hadn't tried any of those touchy-feely "how are you *really* doing?" conversations that his aunts and uncles started every time he'd seen them since Mom's death. He hated those.

His gloomy mood changed the instant he turned

the corner. A red Prius was parked in his driveway. Luke coasted his bike into the garage, dumped it on the floor, and raced into the house.

"Grandmom," he yelled.

She was in the kitchen cooking dinner despite it being seven thirty. After a quick check to make sure his brothers weren't home, he gave his grandmother a hug.

"How's my working boy?" She squeezed him once, then let go. "You've gotten a foot taller at least."

"That's impossible, Grandmom. I saw you last month."

"Well, then I must have shrunk. Now tell me all about this new job of yours. I'm so proud that you had the gumption to get a job this summer. And happy birthday," she cried.

"It's not until tomorrow," he said, hurt that she had forgotten the date, something he would expect from Dad, not Grandmom.

"I know. I wanted to be the first one to tell you." She stirred her steaming pots.

The spicy smell of garlic mixed with a heavy tomato aroma meant she was cooking one of her special Italian dishes. It didn't matter that he'd eaten. His mouth watered in anticipation.

"Where's Dad off to now?" he asked. The arrival of his grandmother usually meant Dad would be gone for awhile.

"North Carolina. Some Boy Scouts are lost in the Smoky Mountains. They needed extra dog teams. He's hoping to be back by Monday or Tuesday."

Dad would miss his birthday. Again. He shouldn't feel disappointed. Dad and Ranger were one of the best SAR teams on the East Coast. Last year they'd rescued a group of lost hikers. Yet Luke needed Dad to do some rescuing at home. Since Mom had died in March, they'd all stumbled through the days like zombies. So far Easter and Mother's Day and the twins' birthday had been painful reminders of the huge hole in their lives, which Dad ignored.

The loud entrance of his brothers interrupted his dark thoughts. They pecked Grandmom's cheek and tried to run off, but she took a firm hold of their hands.

"Wait just a minute. I want to take a look at my blond-haired boys, who are growing into fine young men. You two look just like your father did when he was sixteen." She rambled for a long while.

Luke enjoyed watching his brothers squirm, and he smiled outright when they finally dashed up the stairs.

Grandmom harrumphed as she dumped the cooked spaghetti into a colander. "That'll teach them. Trying to use the old peck-and-run maneuver on me." A puff of steam rose from the sink.

After dinner, Jacob and Scott again bolted upstairs, but this time with the excuse that they had to get ready to go to the movies with friends. Luke clicked on the TV, turning to the Weather Channel. He hadn't checked the weather since this morning and needed to get caught up.

The reek of cologne gagged Luke before his brothers even made it to the bottom step. Grandmom intercepted them at the door with an arsenal of questions and instructions.

"Has your father given you the sex talk yet?" Grandmom demanded.

"*Grandmom*," Jacob cried. His jaw hung open in pure horror.

Luke stuffed a throw pillow into his mouth to stifle

his laughter. If only he had a camera or a cell phone. The shock on Jacob's bright red face would be great for future bribery.

"We're just going with friends. It's not a date." Scott also flushed.

"Still, I think you're old enough to know. If you have a few minutes..."

"Grandmom," they shouted in unison. Nothing could be more embarrassing than having your grandmother offer to teach you the facts of life.

Tears rolled down Luke's cheeks. He hadn't laughed this hard since March.

"Uh, Grandmom, we know all about...that," Scott said, looking everywhere but at her. He noticed Luke on the couch and narrowed his eyes as if zeroing in on a target. "You really need to talk to Luke. He's the one with the girlfriend."

"Am not," Luke shouted, his humor gone in an instant.

"Oh, Megan is *so* great. Oh, Megan is *so* wonderful. She knows *so* much," Scott taunted in a high-pitched voice.

"That's enough, Scott," Grandmom said in *the tone*. The flat, steely voice Dad used with equal success. So that's where Dad had learned it.

When Jacob and Scott left, Grandmom joined him on the couch. Luke liked to see at least a full hour of the Weather Channel, so he knew where all the trouble spots were. Broadening his concern for storms in Dad's flight path, he paid attention to the weather reports for North Carolina as well as the forecast for his home in Hershey, Pennsylvania.

Grandmom kept him company. She asked questions

about the different graphics and clarification about some terms and weather systems. Luke explained it all, glad for the interest, trying not to overanalyze if her interest was fake or not.

"You should be a meteorologist," Grandmom declared.

"What?" Shock shot through him. Was she making a cruel joke?

"You know more about the weather than that guy on TV."

"But that's Jim Cantore."

"Who?"

"That's the guy they send to stand on the beach when a hurricane's barreling in from the Atlantic. He holds his rain hat and his anemometer and tries to look serious, but he's drooling happy because wind speeds are in excess of fifty miles an hour. I mean, palm trees are bending in half, and this guy's standing in front of the camera, reporting that everyone but him has already evacuated." A shiver snaked up Luke's spine. Jim Cantore was The Man.

"You don't have to stand in a hurricane's path to be a meteorologist. You could be the guy that says 'Jim, I predict Hurricane So-and-So will make landfall on the Outer Banks in North Carolina. Go there.'"

Luke laughed. He had always assumed he would work with dogs when he grew up, but now his grandmother had given him something new and scary to think about.

CHAPTER 4

Pond Scum

On Monday morning Luke arrived early. No one was in the kennel, so he walked to the house. Peeking into the sunroom windows, Luke tried to see the puppies. Willajean came in to feed them and noticed him outside. His face burned.

She opened the door. "Come on in, Lost-and-Found. My doors are never locked. You're always welcome." Picking up a steaming mug of coffee, she pointed to the two whelping boxes. "Besides, one of these pups is yours."

The bloodhound puppies had knocked over the metal feeding bowl and were spreading food all over the newspaper-lined floor. They tripped over their own ears as they wrestled with each other. Cute, but not as cute as the tiny, white papillon pups.

Luke leaned over to pet Lady. Smiling, he scratched her behind the ears. The little cotton balls nuzzled their mother, eyes still closed, pink mouths gaping, searching for a nipple to suck.

"Time to feed the dogs," Willajean called.

A chair scraped in the kitchen. Megan came out with powdered sugar crumbs on her lips. She wiped her mouth with her sleeve and followed them to the kennel.

The morning flew by. After all the dogs were fed and put out into the fields, Willajean delayed that afternoon's training session. She had some potential buyers scheduled to look at the bloodhounds. Luke wished they would buy them all, then shook his head. Dad would only make him get one of Mr. Johnson's dogs.

"Hey, Luke, you want to bike to the old dock and have lunch out there?" Megan asked, pulling out a shiny Trek mountain bike.

"Awesome," he said. "Is it new?" He handed her his brown paper lunch bag, and she stuffed it into one of the leather saddlebags over the back wheel.

"Got it in May for my thirteenth birthday." When she strapped on her helmet, its red glitter sparkled in the sunshine.

Luke eyed his rusting hand-me-down bike and nicked helmet. His brothers had trashed their new bikes, uncaring or unconcerned that they'd left Luke with two broken wrecks to piece together into one that worked.

Megan jumped on her bike and sped away on a trail through the forest behind the kennel. Luke struggled to keep up, his thin tires slipping on the dirt path. Familiar with the road, Megan charged and whooped over the bumps and through the underbrush, while Luke stayed on the trail, moving cautiously. She made a sudden right turn. By the time he caught up with her, she was racing down a narrow wooden dock, her wheels drumming on the planks.

"Megan, watch out." The yell exploded from his mouth before he could stifle it. Certain that she would go flying off the end, he dropped his bike on the dirt path and ran after her.

She stopped one plank short of the edge, panting and flushed. "Scared you."

"Did not," he said quickly. "I just didn't want to eat a soggy peanut butter and jelly sandwich."

She laughed and unpacked their lunches. They sat on the edge of the dock with their feet dangling above the pond. Dragonflies zoomed and hovered over the lumpy greenish surface. Insects buzzed in the moist air.

"Mom said you just had a birthday. Any cool stuff?" Megan asked.

"No. Clothes from my grandmom." Luke sighed. He'd needed new clothes. He had outgrown his old ones, and Dad used Jacob and Scott's hand-me-downs for rags. He hated to ask Dad to take him shopping because he didn't want to see the pain in his father's eyes. Clothes shopping had been Mom's job.

Megan crinkled her nose, and Luke guessed it wasn't because of the rotten odor of pond scum from below.

"I hate getting clothes," she said. "I'd rather have a new video game, but my sister loves new outfits. She *lives* for shopping. I'd rather go bike riding. Did you get anything else?"

All he'd gotten from his brothers had been a mumbled "Happy Birthday," while they shoveled down the chocolate cake Grandmom had baked.

"The puppy," he said, wondering if, like clothes that didn't fit, he could exchange it for something he really wanted.

"But that's not really a gift. You're working the summer to pay for it."

"Yeah, but my dad'll be paying for dog food and the vet bills. He'll probably build another bed in the shed for her to use." He sighed again, unable to feel any enthusiasm.

"You don't want a puppy?" Megan stared at him as if he had two heads.

"I don't want a bloodhound pup. I want one of Lady's puppies."

"No problem. My mom wouldn't care. She can sell either. Just let her know."

"It's not that easy."

"Why not?"

Luke shrugged. Megan probably wouldn't understand. Willajean encouraged Megan to think of new ideas for training and to do things differently. If Megan decided she wanted to breed pharaoh hounds, Willajean probably wouldn't have a problem adding a pharaoh hound to her kennel.

"My dad lives and breathes bloodhounds." Luke tried to explain. "He knows everything about them. They're so familiar that any other dog probably seems like an alien from Pluto to him."

Megan laughed, but seeing Luke's glum expression she stopped. "Maybe you can get your dad to like papillons."

"What do you mean?"

"Tell him about how tough and smart they are,

and how much the puppies are worth if you decide to breed your dog. You know, that kind of thing," Megan suggested.

Excitement pulsed in Luke's chest. "I get it. If he knows all about them, and I tell him about all the ribbons Sweetie and Lady have won, he might let me have one."

"If you become an expert on papillons, I'll bet he'll feel better about having one in his house."

"That's a great idea."

Megan's phone chirped. She pulled a red cell phone from her pants pocket, read the text message, and replied. Her thumbs flew over the keyboard.

"A friend?" Luke asked.

"Yeah. Karen, my best friend down in North Carolina." She shoved the phone back into her pocket. "She's biking too. We used to go out all day. I knew all the trails around our houses by heart." Megan tossed a stone into the water. "There are lots of biking trails down there. Up here, I keep running into houses or farms. Do you know any good places to ride?"

"Not really. I stick to the streets."

Megan looked so disappointed, Luke searched his memory. "Oh wait, there's this trail that used to be a railroad track. It goes all the way from Elizabethtown to Mt. Gretna. I think there's an entrance nearby. Oh, and if you go to Mt. Gretna, you have to get ice cream at the Jigger shop. It's the best ever."

"Yeah? Do they have moose tracks? It's my favorite."

"Yep. I always get mint chocolate chip."

"Is it green?"

"Of course, it's not true mint chip if it isn't green."

She laughed, smiling until another text message chirped. "Karen's biking with Becky now, showing her all our secret spots." After she typed, she turned to Luke. "What's your cell number? I'll put it in my contacts."

"I don't have a cell phone."

Megan gasped. "Why not?"

"My dad thinks I don't need one until I'm old enough to drive. That's when my brothers got theirs."

"That's…" Unable to finish, she just gaped at him.

"Crazy, I know. But we don't have a ton of money, and my brothers pay their monthly bill." He shrugged. "I'll give you my home number. Nobody answers that but me."

"But what if—"

"Believe me, I've tried using all the *what-if* situations with my dad. He's stubborn." Luke picked up a pebble and threw it into the water.

"My mom gets that way too. But if I have a good reason, she sees my point. Do you think your dad will let you get a papillon?"

"I don't know." But it was worth a try.

They discussed the best time to approach his dad as they biked back to the kennel. When they drew closer to her farm, Megan stopped and leaned her bike on a tree.

"What's wrong?" Luke pulled next to her.

She gestured to another trail that branched off to the left. Steeper than the one they rode on, it climbed up a hill. "There's an overlook at the top that's awesome. Wanna see?"

"Sure." Luke dumped his bike.

They hiked up the path, huffing in the humid air.

Near the top, Megan pointed straight ahead. "If you keep walking, there a stream that feeds into the pond."

Surprised, Luke asked, "How do you know?"

"I took Lance for a walk, and we found it. I like to

explore the woods around our farm."

"Oh."

She turned to the left and strode down a tight and twisty path. "I missed this turn the first time I hiked up here."

Bushes and leaves scraped along Luke's legs. Briars grabbed his shorts and T-shirt. "Are you sure this is a path?"

"Yeah, it opens up at the end."

As he navigated through the brush, he hoped there wasn't any poison ivy in here. Something about leaves of three –

"Here we are." Megan stepped aside.

Farm fields stretched across the valley like a green sea. "Wow. I can see Hersheypark and the hospital." He stepped onto the rocky outcropping.

"Be careful there's a steep drop-off." Megan warned.

Luke leaned over, peering down. A narrow ledge jutted about ten feet below, but then nothing until the tops of trees at the bottom. Good thing he wasn't afraid of heights. "The view is epic."

"Told you."

They returned to their bikes.

"Maybe the next time you go…er…exploring, you could take me along," Luke said.

"Sure." Megan hopped onto her bike.

"And I'll find out where that Rails-to-Trails thing is for you."

"Great." She peddled off.

Luke followed.

Willajean was waiting for them. "We're going to do a quick training session for these three young dogs. Luke, you work with Hazel, and Megan can deal with Tanner."

Luke and Megan moved to stand next to the dogs.

"Doggie manners are very important," Willajean said. "We'll start with *sit*." She held out a treat. "Easiest way to get a dog to sit is to hold a treat above her nose. Once you have her attention, move it back toward her tail. She'll back up, but eventually she'll sit. And when she does, say *sit* with a commanding tone. Then give her the treat."

Willajean demonstrated with Jackson, a white papillon. It looked easy.

"Another way is to push the dog's back end down, say *sit*, then give the treat. The key is repetition and praise. Your tone helps as well. A wimpy *sit* or a pleading *sit* or one that sounds like all the other words you say won't work. The dog'll just ignore you." She handed treats to Luke and Megan. "All right, you try."

Luke worked with Hazel, a tan bloodhound. She kept jumping up, trying to snatch the treat from his hand.

"Push her down and say *off*. When she stays down, praise her. It might take a few times. Some dogs are smarter than others."

"Sit," Megan ordered Tanner.

His tail hit the ground.

Willajean laughed. "Tanner loves food. He'll do anything for a treat."

After two hours, all three dogs had learned how to sit. Megan took them down to the kennel. Luke walked to the sunroom to visit the puppies again.

Willajean changed the soiled towels in Lady's whelping box for clean ones. "I have buyers for five of the bloodhounds. And that leaves one for me and the other for you." Willajean stuffed the pile of dirty towels into a laundry basket.

Luke leaned over Lady's box, watching the pups. "Willajean?"

"Yes?"

"Could I have one of Lady's pups instead?"

No reply. Too afraid to glance at her, Luke's heartbeat pounded in his ears as he waited.

"I don't have a problem with that. But" – she paused – "you'll have to get permission from your father."

Relief mixed with fear. What if Dad freaked? Luke gnawed on his lip, but decided to go ahead with his plan anyway. Grinning, he scratched Lady behind the ears. "Do you know any papillon websites?"

Willajean huffed. "Wait here." She returned with two books on papillons and handed them to him. "These are better than a website. You can borrow them."

"Thanks." He flipped through the pages. Once he was an expert in all things papillon, he'd talk to Dad.

Luke spent that night and the next studying the books. At one point he had to laugh. He hadn't studied this hard for any of his classes at school. To help him remember, he wrote a list of pros and cons for owning a papillon. Mom would be proud.

Pros: friendly, intelligent, learns fast, adventurous, steady, obedient, not yappy, strong instinct to protect, loves to cuddle, loves outdoor exercise.

Cons: can be possessive of owner, resents outsiders, could also get small-dog syndrome if papillon believes she's the pack leader of the house.

Small-dog syndrome: nervous, high-strung, timid, snapping, biting, barking, and separation anxiety.

Luke reviewed his list. Not bad. The pros far outweighed the cons. And as long as the dog didn't think she was in charge, they could avoid the small-dog syndrome. Soon he'd have enough information to talk to Dad.

When he arrived home on Wednesday, Grandmom said that Dad would be coming home very late, so they'd see him in the morning.

Luke fell asleep with his book resting on his chest and his bedside lamp on. The shrill ring of the phone woke him. He sat up confused. The book slammed to the floor. Who'd turned off his light?

The second ring cut off in midway. Curious about who would call the house phone at four in the morning, Luke padded downstairs.

Phone to his ear, Dad stared out the kitchen window. A suitcase lay on the floor next to the door. He must have just gotten in.

"That's great. I was worried. I'm glad they saved his leg. How's the other little boy?" Dad asked. "Oh, no. Lousy officials with their lousy regulations. They killed that boy. I know, I know. Okay, call me tomorrow. My cell phone should be charged by then. Thanks. Bye." After hanging up, Dad reached up and opened the cabinet above the refrigerator. He pulled out a dark brown bottle and poured a drink.

A bad rescue.

Dad never drank the hard stuff except when upset. He drank himself to sleep every night for two months after Mom died. And when he'd returned from Japan after the earthquake.

Dad grunted when he noticed Luke in the doorway.

"Thought the phone would wake you. Your brothers would sleep through a tornado." Slumping in one of the kitchen chairs, he gestured for Luke to join him. Then he took a long pull from his glass. The lines on his face drooped like a bloodhound's ears.

"The world is full of idiots," he said to Luke. "Twenty kids lost in the woods for a week. Squadrons of men marching and searching in the wrong direction for six days." He took another gulp. "Finally, they call in dog teams. After *six* days." He waved six fingers in the air.

"They'd filled the woods with their stench, so it took us a couple days to determine their search area was way off beam. After that it took only a day to find those boys." He slammed his glass on the table. Squinting at Luke as if he were actually seeing him for the first time, Dad lowered his voice. "They were in bad shape. Starving, thirsty, a couple kids with sprained ankles. One kid had fallen off a cliff and busted his leg. Kids your age." Dad swallowed hard, his eyes welling with tears. "One boy didn't make it. If they'd called in the dogs right away, Ranger would have found them before their first hunger pangs. Idiots." His father drained the glass and poured himself another drink.

Luke sat as still as a rabbit caught in Hounddog's teeth. Normally Dad never talked about the searches that ended badly.

As if reading his mind, Dad said, "Luke, I'm telling you this for a very important reason. You might not want to do search and rescue with your dog, but think about it. The more qualified teams there are, the better. Jacob and Scott will soon be able to help me. Even if you don't train your dog, we can breed her with Ranger, and maybe she'll whelp smart puppies that can be trained for search and rescue."

His father's face sagged, and dark circles of exhaustion hung under his eyes.

Blinking several times as if trying to hold back tears, Dad said, "Someday, when he's too old to run up mountains hot on the scent, I'll have to replace Ranger."

Luke hunkered down in his chair, crushed by grief and unable to breathe. Dad loved his dog almost as much as he loved Mom. She'd teased Dad about it all the time. He'd smile and laugh, but never deny it.

"I'm tired." Dad rubbed the stubble on his chin. "I'm going to bed." Setting his glass in the sink, he grabbed his suitcase and headed upstairs.

Luke sat in the kitchen for a long time. Had his dad checked in on him and seen the papillon book? Someone had turned off his light, but that seemed more of a grandmom thing. Either way, how could he ask for a papillon now?

Dad had good reasons, too. Getting a papillon was like buying a candy bar. Luke might want it with all his heart, but he didn't need it to survive. It'd be selfish to own a dog just because Mom had thought a papillon would be perfect for Luke. After all, she wouldn't be disappointed in him for giving into Dad. Right?

When the sky lightened, Luke dragged himself to bed and slept until noon.

Later on Thursday afternoon, Luke biked slowly to Willajean's. He decided to do the mature thing and get a bloodhound. Determined to at least fake a positive attitude, he parked his bike next to the training area.

He hopped over the fence, then stopped short. Working next to Megan was another girl. And not just some ordinary farm girl. This girl's hair was styled, her clothes matched, and she wore makeup. The teenager stood out amid the dogs and training equipment like a pampered poodle in a group of junkyard hounds.

She thrust a harness into Megan's arms, shrilling an order. When Megan failed to respond, the new girl turned to see what had Megan's attention.

"Who's that?" Her fire-red lips twisted into a sneer.

"That's Luke." Megan waved him over. "Luke, this is my sister, Alayna."

"Hey," he said.

Alayna eyed his ripped shorts and stained T-shirt. She squinted and gave him a pained smile. "Didn't my mother call you?" She spoke as if he were dimwitted.

"About what?" His good mood dissolved under Alayna's icy stare.

She rolled her eyes. "I'm working here now," she said slowly. "Mother doesn't need your help anymore." Alayna sighed dramatically at his confusion. "Go home." She waved painted fingernails in the direction of his bike. "You're fired."

CHAPTER 5

Serial Killer
from the Sky

Alayna's words shocked him speechless.

"Don't listen to her, Luke," Megan said. "Mom told her she can work here *temporarily* until she finds another job. You're not fired."

The blockage in his throat eased slightly at Megan's words, but Alayna had set her jaw in a determined – or maybe calculating – line. Luke couldn't be sure.

"I plan to stay," she said. Once again she appraised him with her gaze. Her painted fingernails seemed to elongate and curve into claws. A cunning cat among friendly dogs, she was likely to scratch without notice. "He won't last."

Before Luke or Megan could reply, Willajean swept

into the training yard. She issued instructions with her usual no-nonsense attitude, starting the afternoon's session. When the drills were set up, Willajean let the three of them work the dogs as she headed back toward the house.

"Guide the dog like *this*," Alayna said, snapping the lead hard into Luke's hands.

The leather stung his palms, but the burning wasn't as painful as her words.

"Come *on*. Don't you know anything about dogs? Thank God, I'm back. Poor mother must have been beside herself having to work with *you*. A charity case for sure." Alayna pushed him aside and snatched the leash from his hands. "Follow me, Dog Boy, if you want to learn something."

Luke shot a pleading look at Megan. She shrugged. Alayna had been bossing her around too, but if it bothered Megan, she didn't show it. She ignored Alayna, but he couldn't. He was new to dog training, and like it or not, Alayna had experience.

Besides, if he upset Alayna, she'd whine about it to Willajean. If it came down to Alayna or Luke, he had a pretty good idea who would be staying and who would be home alone all day watching the Weather Channel.

Suppressing a sigh, Luke followed Alayna, helping her with the drills. She used the same quick, efficient commands as her mother, but she lacked the warmth. To Alayna, the dogs were an item on a "To Do" list. Get dog out of kennel, put dog through training, put dog back in kennel. No praise for a good job. No hugs. No scratches behind the ears.

"Megan, stop that. You're wasting time," Alayna scolded.

Megan was wrestling with Lance. He'd finished the track without errors. Again. Lance was the Einstein of the dog world. Brushing the dirt off her pants, Megan returned to work. But whenever Alayna wasn't watching, she played with the dogs.

As the day progressed, Alayna kept getting on Luke's case. In her eyes, he did everything wrong. She called him Dog Boy a zillion times. His frustration turned to anger.

A brisk breeze blew from the east, and a dark line of clouds crept in from the west. The thick black bases and tall white pillars of clouds sucked in the warm moist air as it advanced, feeding the storm.

Oh no. In a heartbeat, fear replaced his anger. The Weather Channel hadn't predicted a thunderstorm. The wind increased as big fat raindrops struck the ground. Panic pulsed in his chest.

Alayna ran for the house, leaving Megan and Luke to take the dogs to the kennel. Megan held the door wide as Luke ushered them into the building.

When all the dogs were settled in their crates, Luke and Megan prepared the food for the next day in the kennel's kitchen. Luke jumped every time thunder exploded in the air. Rain drummed on the roof at the same tempo that his hands shook as he tried to chop onions and carrots. He didn't dare look at Megan, afraid of her expression, afraid of her questions.

After they finished with the food, Megan suggested they make a run for the house.

"Not safe," Luke said.

"Why not?"

"Lightning. The serial killer from the sky."

"What?" Megan put her hands on her hips and

peered at him as if he'd lost his mind.

"More than seven thousand Americans have been killed by lightning in the past fifty years," Luke said with authority. He might not be an expert when it came to dogs, but he knew all about thunderstorms.

"Yeah, right. Like that's going to happen here." She took a step toward the door.

"We have to walk across the lawn to get to the house. We would be the tallest objects. Lightning always strikes the tallest object." Talking helped calm Luke's racing heart, and his anxiety eased a little when Megan moved away from the door.

"Are you planning to be a weatherman when you grow up?" Megan asked. "That would be cool." She joined Luke, who stood as far from the windows and doors as was physically possible.

"I don't know. Maybe." Luke shrugged. "I could be a meteorologist."

"A *meteo* what? Is that like studying meteors?" Megan's dark eyebrows creased together.

"Not meteors from outer space. More like hydrometeors." Seeing no comprehension in her brown eyes, Luke explained. "Raindrops. A meteorologist studies the weather."

Megan punched him in the arm. "You're as bad as Mr. Phillips, my dorky science teacher, using all those fancy words." She smiled, letting Luke know she was just kidding.

"Do you like science?" he asked.

"Kinda." She glanced around. "Some stuff is cool, like the units on biology. But that class has stuff we'll never use."

"Yeah. What's the point of memorizing the genus,

species, and all those other names when we can look it up on the Internet?"

She agreed. "It's a complete waste of time."

The lights flickered, and Luke held his breath until they steadied. Because the storm showed no signs of letting up, Megan let Lance out of his crate. Although she'd never said as much, Luke figured Lance was her favorite. She fed him first, and she played with him the most.

The German shepherd plopped down next to her on the floor and laid his big head in her lap. She scratched him behind the ears, while he grunted in contentment. Lance's ability to learn fast made him a perfect dog for SAR. He'd probably pass all the certification tests without trouble.

As if reading his thoughts, Megan asked, "Do you ever go out with your dad when he's on a search-and-rescue mission?"

"No." Luke reached over and petted Lance. "I'm too young. He won't even let Jacob and Scott go, at least not yet. He keeps promising them he'll take them, but..." He shrugged, too embarrassed to explain his dad's obsession with search and rescue. Having two inexperienced teenagers tagging along would certainly slow him down. "He took us to a SAR open house once, and I learned a few basics about how to handle an emergency situation. It was pretty cool," Luke said.

"It must be great having a hero as a father," Megan said wistfully, her gaze focused on a distant point.

"Hero?" Luke had never thought of Dad that way.

"Sure. Rescuing people who might have died. That's up there with firefighters and police officers."

Luke squirmed. "What does your father do?"

Megan's face darkened as if he had invited the storm into the kennel. Luke immediately regretted the question.

"He's lower than a deer tick on a dog's butt." She spat the words out. "You don't think your father's a hero? Then you should meet my father." Megan took a breath, and Luke braced for a deluge.

"Never around, always off with some skank. We thought he'd gotten his money from dealing drugs, but it's worse than that." Megan's hands pressed into Lance's back. The dog didn't seem to mind the extra hard rub.

"The last time I saw my father, he was arguing with my mom. He stormed off that night, and the next day all the puppies were gone. Mom had twelve bloodhounds and eight German shepherd pups ready to sell." She leaned over and rubbed her cheek on Lance's head.

"He sold them to one of those research labs that experiments on animals. He was their supplier and had been making a living by stealing dogs."

She wiped her face and straightened. Flicking her hands out from her body as if she were pushing the bad feelings away, she said, "Mom called the police, and we never saw him again."

Luke thought about the twelve puppies in Willajean's sunroom. What if they disappeared? It'd be awful.

"You think he would ever show up here?" Luke asked.

"If he does, I'll sic Lance on him. Right, boy? You'll get him."

Lance thumped his tail on the floor and gazed at Megan with his adoring brown eyes. "At least you'll knock him over in your enthusiasm. Get his pants dirty, that'll piss him off." Megan scowled, then stood up without warning. She led Lance back to his crate. "Storm's over. See you tomorrow."

"I guess," Luke said to the closing door. Facing Alayna at seven in the morning would suck. As he biked slowly through the wet streets, he hoped he hadn't ruined his friendship with Megan by asking about her father.

Saying or doing something stupid. Fact of life.

CHAPTER 6

Dog Boy

Luke's nightmare turned into reality when he opened the kennel door. Seven a.m. Friday morning, and there stood Alayna in her makeup and color-coordinated glory, dishing out dog food. *Oh no.* Willajean was nowhere in sight.

"You're late," Alayna said when she spotted him in the doorway. The clock on the wall read 7:01. "Come on, Dog Boy." She shoved a bowl of food into his hands. "Get your lazy butt moving. We have work to do."

Alayna kept up a brisk pace. Luke and Megan hustled to deliver the food, and all the dogs were fed in half the time it usually took. After they'd cleaned up the kitchen, Alayna pointed to the dogs' runs. "Scoop poop, Luke." She laughed hard at her own joke, but when Megan moved to go with him she said, "You don't shovel poop. That's what Dog Boy is here for." She pulled Megan with her.

Megan mouthed the word *sorry* as the door shut. Luke slammed the gates, letting the dogs out of their runs and into the fields. Fuming, he banged his scraper against the metal fences. He imagined rubbing Alayna's face into the bucket of dog droppings. The picture of her makeup smeared with smelly poop made Luke laugh out loud.

"Oh, Alayna," he said, pretending. "It matches your dung-brown hair and your dirt-brown eyes perfectly."

Willajean made a brief appearance that afternoon to help set up the training. To Luke's dismay, she left the three of them to work the dogs while she went back to the house to make phone calls.

"Don't hold the lead that tight," Alayna corrected him during one run.

Then later, "The scent pads should be at least six feet apart, Dog Boy."

And, "Did you take a nap? I sent you to fetch Roulette *ages* ago."

Alayna continued to pick on him all afternoon. He'd say she treated him like one of the dogs, but she treated the dogs better.

"Are you hard of hearing, or just stupid, Dog Boy?" She snatched a leash from Luke's hands.

That's enough. Luke turned his back on her.

"Where do you think you're going?" Alayna demanded.

Luke hunched his shoulders and kept walking toward the house. Unsure of how long he could endure

Alayna's taunts, he wanted to see the puppies before he either gave in and quit, or Willajean asked him to leave.

His gloomy mood scattered at the sight of the frolicking, clumsy bloodhound puppies. Willajean joined him in the sunroom, and he helped her clean out the newspapers in the two whelping boxes. He picked up one of Lady's little pups. Holding the white fur ball in one hand, he rubbed the puppy's back with a finger.

"I just got a call about that last bloodhound pup. Have you talked to your dad yet?" Willajean asked.

He kept his gaze on the pup. "No. He just got back."

"Can you let me know tomorrow?"

"Sure," Luke mumbled. He put the puppy back in the box. Holding the pup felt like carrying an ice-cream cone on a hot day and not being able to have a lick.

To make matters worse, Alayna burst into the sunroom.

"There you are," she said to Luke. Accusation burned in her eyes. "He left us to finish the training," she whined to her mother. "He doesn't even know how to train a dog. We don't need him. Megan and I did fine without him."

"Alayna," Willajean said sternly, "Luke and I have a business deal. He's doing fine. If you're not happy, I suggest you find another babysitting job."

Luke wanted to dance an *in-your-face* jig at Alayna, but her bright red lips snapped together as a stubborn line appeared along her jaw. She shot him a glare full of venom that promised revenge. Spinning on her heels, she stomped out.

Willajean shook her head. "Don't mind her, Luke. She's upset about losing her job. Since it's late June, all the summer positions have been taken. So she's stuck here."

Luke didn't know what to say. He glanced out the window. Megan was struggling to get all the dogs into the kennel by herself.

"I'd better go help Megan," he said.

Luke spent the rest of the week enduring Alayna's taunts and avoiding Willajean. He should tell her to keep a bloodhound pup for him, but he couldn't say the words.

An unwelcome sight greeted him Friday night when he arrived home. His brothers had commandeered the living room. Jacob and Scott were watching a movie with their loud, obnoxious friends, while Dad relaxed on his recliner, laughing with Scott over a rude joke.

"Hey, Pooper Scooper's home," Jacob said. "Tell Levi here that you're scooping poop for your summer job. He doesn't believe me."

Ignoring them, Luke headed for the stairs. If he stayed, he would become the target of every joke. When they had company, Jacob and Scott didn't want their little brother hanging around.

Luke tried to read the dog training books. But unable to concentrate, he turned on his weather radio to cover the rowdy noise from downstairs. Half listening to the forecast, Luke flipped through the pages, scanning the words. He couldn't find a comfortable position on the bed, so he moved to his desk. Propping his feet on top was too high, so he pulled out a bottom drawer, but his chair was too hard.

Finally, Luke took a notebook from his desk and

wrote another list of positive reasons for owning a papillon. Despite Dad's desire for another bloodhound, Luke decided to ask him if he could have one of Lady's pups anyway. If Dad said *no*, at least he'd tried.

When Dad came up to deliver a couple slices of pizza for dinner, Luke pounced. "Dad, can I talk to you about something?"

"Sure, buddy, but not right now. I want to see the end of the movie." His dad waved as he closed Luke's bedroom door.

Luke tried all weekend to get Dad alone. He suggested going to a movie or the mall. Car rides were good for conversations because there wasn't that whole eye-contact thing going on. But Dad was too busy fixing stuff around the house or working in the dogs' shed.

The shed was his father's masterpiece. Jacob had painted *The Puppy Palace* on the shed door after Dad had installed bunk beds, windows, a ceiling fan, baseboard heaters, and had personalized food and water dishes for each of the three dogs. The boys had been stunned by the effort. Mom had teased Dad about how their own house was falling apart, but the Palace gleamed with three coats of paint.

Sunday afternoon when Dad took Jacob and Scott out to train their dogs, they left Luke behind to clean up the mess in the kitchen. Not invited to go along, Luke stalked around the room as his anger simmered. He tossed the juice glasses into the dishwasher, hoping they'd shatter, but they landed without even cracking.

The newspaper was strewn around the kitchen. Luke smashed the different sections into balls and slam-dunked them into the trashcan. The help-wanted ads caught his eye before he could crush them. His mood improved as he scanned the ads, picturing Alayna working in various positions. Hair-washing assistant. Drive-through-window clerk. Telemarketing operator. Remembering the comment Willajean had made, he saved the ads as an idea swirled in his mind.

Luke vowed to corner Dad by the end of the day, but he'd forgotten it was pinochle night. Once again Dad headed out the door. Luke kicked the wall. Not once all weekend had Dad spent time with him. Dad knew he wanted to talk and was purposely avoiding him.

Fine, then. I'll make my own decision.

After a restless night, Luke ate his cereal. He read the help-wanted ads again. When his brothers came in, he tried to put the paper away, but Scott noticed the furtive movement and pounced.

"What's this?" Scott yanked the paper from Luke. "Pooper Scooper is having delusions of grandeur. Thinks he's qualified for another job."

"I'm sure he could find employment as a port-a-potty cleaner or men's room attendant," Jacob said.

His appetite gone, Luke pushed away from the table. Grabbing his paper from Scott, he shot a sour look at Dad, who was engrossed in the morning newspaper.

Luke left without another word and biked hard to Willajean's. With each push on the pedals, he debated. Left foot down, confront Alayna. Right foot down, ignore her. Left foot, tell Willajean the truth and be stuck with a bloodhound. Right foot, lie for now, but change Dad's mind so it would be true later. Left. Right. Left. Right. The bike's tires hummed on the asphalt.

Arriving at the kennel five minutes early, Luke sucked in a deep breath and smoothed the newspaper before going inside.

"Let's hustle, Dog Boy, we don't have all day," Alayna said.

"I hear McDonald's is hiring. They have flexible summer hours and will accommodate your schedule when you return to school," Luke said. He took the bowl from her hands and left before she could reply.

After that, whenever Alayna called him Dog Boy, he quoted help-wanted ads. Megan covered her mouth to stifle her laughter.

Later, Alayna said, "Okay, Dog Boy, time to pick up poop."

"The beauty parlor around the corner's looking for a shop assistant. I hear they give discounts to their employees."

"What's your problem, Dog Boy?" Alayna finally asked.

"My name is Luke." He waved the help-wanted ads in Alayna's face. "And if you don't stop calling me 'Dog Boy' and be nicer to me, I'm going to show these ads to your mom so she knows there are still plenty of summer jobs you can apply for."

Alayna's eyes blazed. "You wouldn't dare." Her glitter-gold fingernails disappeared as she clenched her hands into fists.

Scary, but not as scary as his brothers. "Try me." Luke matched her defiant stare.

Finally, she whirled around. "Megan, come," she ordered.

"No. I'm going to help Luke," Megan said.

Nice. He shot her a thumbs-up behind Alayna's back. When Alayna stormed out, Luke sagged against the counter. *Yes!* Fist pump.

Megan clapped him on the back. "Awesome. That

should shut her up."

"I wasn't sure it would work." He grinned.

"Why not? You're a genius."

"Yeah, right. You haven't seen my grades for English and history."

"Can't be as bad as mine." Megan grabbed a metal scraper. "English is the worst. First you get all these rules and then all these exceptions to the rules. It gives me a headache. Math makes more sense."

"You like math?" Luke entered a run.

"Not really, but I'm good at it."

"What did you take at your old school?"

"Algebra. Mom signed me up for geometry this year. I'll probably be the only new kid and eighth grader in the class." She sighed.

"There's a bunch of other eighth grade math geeks, including me, so you won't be alone."

"Cool."

"But you'll probably be the only new student."

"I figured. I'm already dreading the first day of school." Megan dumped her piles into the bucket. "Being stared at on the bus…"

"You don't have to take the bus. You can bike to school if the weather's nice. We could go together… I have to pass your house anyway…" Heat spread up his back, but Luke kept his gaze on the ground.

"That'd be great. Thanks."

The afternoon's training session went smoothly. Alayna refused to speak to Luke, which suited him just fine. After preparing the food for the next day,

Luke followed Megan to the house to visit the pups. He wasn't there long before Willajean asked him about the bloodhound pup.

"Go ahead and sell it," Luke said. "Dad agreed to the papillon." A ball of nausea churned up his throat. He petted the white pup in his hands, hoping somehow it would work out, that he would convince Dad.

Willajean was quiet for awhile. Then she said, "That's good. I'll call right now."

His chest tightened as Willajean talked on the phone. By the time she returned to the sunroom, he regretted his rashness. *Dad's gonna freak.*

"All set," Willajean said with satisfaction. "Storm Watcher Kennel is having a good summer."

To take his mind off the bloodhound pup, he asked, "Why did you name it *Storm Watcher*?"

Willajean paused for a moment, pursing her lips. "Well, every time a thunderstorm blew in, my father and I sat on the back porch and watched the lightning strikes move closer until the pouring rain forced us inside." She picked up a puppy and stroked his wriggling body.

"I never knew how much my dad liked the weather until he died and I found thirty years of weather data in his desk. Then I discovered a tower way out in the back cornfield. It has instruments to measure wind speed and direction, temperature, and rainfall."

She had a weather tower? Sweet. Luke would love to see it. The back cornfield must be pretty far away, or he'd have noticed it before.

Putting the dog down, Willajean gazed out the window for so long that Luke thought she had finished.

"I guess I named the kennel after my father. Funny," she muttered more to herself than to Luke, "I didn't realize that until now."

Willajean shook her head as if to push away her father's memory, but then stopped as if she'd had a sudden idea. "Wait here." She hurried out.

Luke continued to pet the pup on his lap, wondering what had lit a fire under her.

Willajean poked her head back into the room. "Come on." She jingled keys in her hand.

"Where?" Luke set the pup into the box.

"You'll see."

CHAPTER 7

Why Not?

Luke followed Willajean out back. She jumped into a golf cart. He had barely enough time to sit next to her before she stomped on the gas.

"Megan told me you know all about the weather."

"Not everything." Luke clutched the seat as she made a sharp turn.

"But you're interested in it. Right?"

"I guess."

"See that ridge?" Willajean pointed across the fields as she drove. "When dark clouds gathered above that ridge, my dad knew a storm was brewing, and no matter what he was doing, he'd stop and find me. We'd sit on the big yellow swing and watch the lightning flicker and flash. My dad used to say it was Morse code, that the storm was signaling his buddies." Willajean chuckled, her gaze on the distant ridge.

"Then the cornstalks would dance in the wind while thunder boomed and rumbled. When the storm became a full fury, it rolled into the valley like a boulder gaining speed down a mountain, soaking everything in its path."

Luke scanned the ridge, relieved by the bright blue above. No sign of black clouds. Didn't Willajean's dad know how dangerous it was to be outside during a thunderstorm? Should he tell her?

No. A half smile of remembrance curved Willajean's lips. Luke recognized that smile. Every time his grandmother reminisced about Mom, she wore that same mixed expression.

At the end of the field, Willajean drove through a tight gap in a line of bushes and trees. Luke had assumed that was the back edge of her farm, but on the other side was another cornfield. Willajean slowed the golf cart as she wove through the field, avoiding the foot-high plants. A metal tower glinted in the sun.

Luke gawked. *Is that an anemometer and wind vane at the top?*

The neat green rows parted and circled around the guide wires at the base of the structure. Following a thin dirt path, Willajean drove right up to the tower. She stopped the cart and hopped out. Luke joined her.

Wow. Pretty cool. Luke had never expected to see a weather tower out in the middle of a cornfield.

Blocking the sun from his eyes, he craned his neck to peer at the top. He'd been right. A three-cupped anemometer spun weakly in the light breeze. The wind wasn't strong enough to push the vane in the right direction.

"This weather station hasn't worked since my dad got sick." Willajean pulled a handful of soggy leaves from a white bucket at the base of the tower.

Probably a rain gauge.

"I'd like to get it back up and running, but I haven't a clue how to do it. Would you like to try?" she asked.

He stepped back. "Me?"

"Sure, why not? It's not like you can break it."

He examined the tower. About thirty feet high, its triangular shape resembled three metal ladders hooked together. The wires from the two instruments on top snaked down one of the legs and disappeared into a white plastic box. Wires from the rain gauge and from a temperature sensor also led into the box. Inside the box, all the wires connected to what he guessed was a data logger or computer. He searched for the power source. A small solar panel had been attached about halfway up the tower.

"Do you still have the instruction manuals for the instruments?" he asked.

"My father never threw anything out. I'm sure they're in his desk somewhere. Does that mean you'll give it a try?"

Luke's gut instinct had been to say *no way*, but the thrill of a challenge stirred in him. He smiled. "Sure, why not?"

"That's the spirit." She tossed the golf cart's keys to Luke. "You drive."

He caught the keys. "Me?" Fear replaced his excitement.

"Yes, you."

"But, I don't know—"

"Have you ever driven the bumper cars at Hersheypark?" she asked.

"Yeah, but—"

"This is the same thing. Come on." Willajean settled into the passenger seat.

Luke hesitated, but joined her and started the engine. Driving slowly, he gripped the steering wheel tightly. But Willajean encouraged him to loosen up. He relaxed a bit, increasing the speed. They bumped over ruts and splashed through puddles. By the time they reached the house, Luke couldn't stop grinning.

The afternoon's training session had finished, and Luke helped Megan settle the dogs and chop the vegetables for the next day. When they were done, he wanted to see the tower again, so he and Megan rode their bikes out to the back cornfield.

Megan pulled a notepad and pencil from the pack on her bike and handed them to Luke. She scowled into the sunlight. "More work," she said.

"What?" Luke sketched the tower and the location of the weather instruments.

"If Mom gets this thing working, I'm going to be running out here two or three times a week recording weather data."

"Have you done it before?" Luke asked.

"Yeah. Poppy used to make me come here and write stuff down whenever we came to visit." Megan popped the door open to the data logger. "See this button? I'd press it and different red numbers showed up on this screen." She pointed. "Poppy thought I'd be excited to have my own job on the farm. It was our secret because he didn't want my mom to know he spent money on his hobby. That's why he hid it way out here, but—" She shrugged. "I liked animals better than these gizmos."

"Do you miss him?" Luke asked, distracted from his sketch.

"He was cranky, smelly, and as stubborn as a terrier after a rat. He was ancient. Old people die." Megan kicked the dirt. A pale yellow puff mushroomed around her feet.

She turned her back to Luke. After the way she'd gotten mad about her dad, he wasn't about to push it. He continued drawing and almost didn't hear what she said next.

"Yeah, I miss him."

Her words were as quiet as the rustle of the cornstalks in the wind. He wanted to tell her he knew how she felt, but his throat refused to work. He'd heard that soulless expression too many times in the last five months. It gave no comfort. It changed nothing. Empty funeral words.

His pencil snapped in two. Relaxing his grip on the broken piece, Luke tried to concentrate on the picture. This drawing of the tower's set up would help him when he read the instrument manuals.

By the time he and Megan rode back to the house, the sun had turned into a bloated orange hovering over the horizon. As promised, Willajean had dug out the manuals, and Megan lent Luke her backpack to carry them home.

When he arrived home, his father had left him a dinner plate in the refrigerator. Luke heated it up in the microwave. Dad only cooked beef. Burgers, steak on the grill, or a roast in the oven were his mainstays. Otherwise Dad ordered pizza or fast food. Luke never thought he'd miss vegetables in a million years, but he did. Vegetables meant someone cared about him.

Luke spread the instrument manuals out on the table and read them while munching on his burger and soggy fries. He was almost done when the door banged open. Ranger raced through the kitchen, followed by Dad.

"Late night?" he asked Luke.

"Yeah. Willajean gave me a new project."

Dad peered over his shoulder, then picked up the wind-speed manual.

"She's got a weather tower on her farm. She wants me to try to fix it." Luke held his breath, waiting for Dad to laugh at the absurdity of someone asking a kid to repair a weather sensor. His father was an electrician, and he'd never once asked Luke or his brothers to help him install an outlet. Mom used to say that Dad didn't have the patience, but Luke believed he just didn't have the interest.

Instead of laughing, Dad flipped through the books. "These sensors all generate an electrical signal. And this logger," he said, pointing, "records the signals and calculates the data."

Now that Luke had his dad's attention, he jumped at the opportunity to ask him questions about how to restart the weather station.

"First thing you need to do is clean everything," Dad said.

"Everything?"

"Yep. Sometimes the culprit is just plain old dirt. It clogs things up and interferes with electrical contact points."

Dad sat next to him and made notes on the sketch

of the tower. "Check the data logger's battery and all the wires, every inch, to see if they're in good condition." He drummed the pencil's eraser on the table. "Wait a minute."

He left the kitchen. When he came back, he had a box filled with tools. Jacob and Scott followed him, and Luke suppressed a groan. Something else for them to tease him about. But they surprised him by being interested. First time in months.

"Here's some cleaner that should work, and my ohm meter to check the battery." Dad explained the different tools he'd put in the box.

Luke marveled at his brothers and father. They were acting like a family again, like they had before Mom died. Unfortunately, it didn't last long.

Jacob and Scott thought it would be cool to have a tower in their backyard.

"Think of the advantages, Dad," Jacob said. "You would be able to calibrate the wind speed by how far back the dogs' ears blow. That way, when you're out in the woods, you would know the exact wind conditions. Like if Ranger's ears were full back that might equal twenty-miles-per-hour wind speeds."

"Mom would've loved it," Scott said. "Remember how she never checked the weather? With a weather station in the backyard, she'd have known the exact temperature outside. Instead of shivering during all those dog trials, she would have been prepared."

Scott's big smile, though, wilted when Dad didn't join in the laughter. Dad's whole body stiffened. All animation drained from his face as if someone had switched him off.

"Time for bed," he said. Each word an effort. He

shuffled out of the room, dragging all the good feelings with him.

Luke sagged in his chair. Scott had to mention Mom. Reminiscing about her was taboo. Not because Dad had ever said so, but because every time she was mentioned, Dad bolted for his bedroom.

"Without Dad there to help you, you'll never get the tower working, Weather Weenie." Jacob's harsh words hammered into the silence.

"Better stick to scooping poop. It's more suitable for your level of intelligence," Scott said.

After a few more taunts, they left the kitchen. Luke should have been hurt, especially after their earlier nice remarks. But the quick change in their mood snagged in his brain. And teetering just out of reach was the answer to why his brothers constantly teased him. After a moment, it clicked.

They blamed him for Mom's death.

CHAPTER 8

The Calm Before the Storm

Guilt poured over him like a cooler filled with icy soda. No surprise Jacob and Scott blamed him. Luke had caused Mom's death, but he hadn't connected the mean teasing with it. That was their way of punishing him. They'd been like this ever since the night his seventh-grade homeroom had won a free screening at the movies by collecting the most canned goods for the food drive. Halfway through the movie, thunder rumbled loud enough to be heard over the soundtrack.

He'd panicked and called Mom to come get him. "Now, please," he'd said.

Mom had never arrived to take him home.

Lightning had struck, and she'd died on her way to the movie theater. On her way to pick him up early.

Luke drew in a shaky breath. Leaving the instrument manuals on the table, he crawled into bed without changing. He huddled under the blanket. Dad must hate him too. That must be why Dad let the twins torment him.

It was a long miserable night, tossing and turning and wondering what he should do. Apologize? Talk to Dad? Would it change anything? No.

Nothing would bring Mom back. Nothing.

But would it change how Jacob and Scott treated him? Would it make Dad pay more attention to him? Wasn't Dad already spending more time with him now that they had Willajean's weather tower? Why ruin it? His thoughts spun like a puppy chasing her tail.

By morning, Luke couldn't think about it anymore. If he did, he'd go insane and never leave his bed. Plus Storm Watcher kennel was the one place he felt almost normal. Almost.

July turned out to be the quiet before the storm. Every afternoon for an hour, Luke worked on the weather instruments and, at the same time, avoided Alayna. Fun. At night he sat at the kitchen table with Dad. They discussed the tower and planned what he should do to fix the instruments.

By early July the corn plants had doubled in size. After climbing up and down the tower twice, Luke dripped with sweat. He stopped for a drink. When a warm sponge pressed against the back of his leg, he dropped his water bottle in surprise and spun around.

Lance sat on the dirt path. The dog had nosed him. His bushy tail swept the ground, creating a plume of dust.

At least he didn't jump on me. He's learned something.

Lance's brown eyes held a cocky glint. The dog looked mighty pleased with himself. Luke scanned the cornfield, searching for Willajean.

Ten minutes later, Megan arrived, red-faced. Her short hair clung to her sweaty forehead.

"There he is," Megan said between huffs. "I don't know whether to praise him or punish him."

"What do you mean?"

"He's not supposed to be here. We were playing, and I said your name. It was weird. He stood real still with his nose up, and then he just took off."

Luke glanced at the wind vane. He was upwind of the training yard. "Why did you say my name?"

"Oh." Megan stammered, and the red splotches on her face spread. "I said maybe when Luke comes back, we might take him swimming in the pond."

"I think praise. You said my name, and he found me. Isn't that what your mom's training him to do?"

"I guess. But he shouldn't have bolted." She sighed. "He's still a pup. I don't want to be too hard on him." Megan scratched Lance behind the ears, telling him he'd did good. He leaned against her legs.

"If you help me finish, we can detour to the pond on the walk back," Luke said.

"Okay."

They worked for awhile in silence. Lance snuffled through the corn, flushing out a couple of rabbits. He chased them into the tree line and then looped back to check on Megan and Luke before racing back into the corn to investigate again.

"I'm going to ask Mom if I can have him," Megan said.

Luke was so focused on the wind speed sensor that he had to stop and think. "Have who?"

"Lance. Mom's training him to do search and rescue. I really want to do it. To be his partner. There's a ton of training involved. If I start now while he's a puppy, by the time I'm sixteen, we'll both be ready to volunteer with a SAR team."

"What're your chances that she'll agree?" Luke remembered his unsuccessful attempt to get permission for a papillon.

"She's fond of Lance, but if I show her I know what I'm getting into, I might convince her that I'm serious. Just like you did with your dad. Right? And that worked out."

"Yeah," Luke said. He ignored the queasy pinch in his gut. The desire to confess to Megan that he hadn't gotten permission from Dad pushed up his throat. Luke had been afraid to say anything to Dad. Megan might have an idea, a solution to his dilemma, but he swallowed the words.

When they finished, they took Lance to the pond. He raced to the edge of the dock, dog-flopped into the water, and splashed Luke and Megan. It must have felt good on his hot skin. Luke would have jumped in after him, but pond scum clung to the banks.

"Here's a perfect stick for him." Megan threw it over Lance's head.

Lance surged after it. He clamped the stick in his teeth and swam back to the dock. Dripping wet, Lance scrambled up the bank and plopped the stick onto Megan's work boots. Just as she reached down to grab it,

Lance shook his body, spraying her with water. The dog had a mischievous streak.

Luke laughed. "Good dog."

Megan yelled, "Bad dog." But she couldn't keep a straight face.

"So when are you going to ask your mom about Lance?" Luke asked.

"When she's in a really good mood." Megan launched the stick high into the air. "Probably before the bloods go to their new owners. She's always moody when a litter leaves. But I think, why get sad? You can't run a kennel if you keep all the dogs. Fact of life."

Luke understood. It hurt to let go of something you loved. And despite her flippant *fact-of-life* comment, he suspected Megan understood too.

After Lance tired, they walked back to the kennel. The other dogs had already been returned to their crates. Luke peeked through the kitchen window. Alayna hacked carrots for the dogs' food with furious strokes.

"I'd better head home now," Luke said.

"Coward," Megan chided.

"I'm not the one who ran off and left her with all the work."

Megan swung her arm to swat him. Luke ducked, and she missed him by inches. She stepped toward him.

"Later." Wagging his fingers, he sprinted for his bike and jumped on.

She stopped chasing him half way up the lane.

"Coward," she shouted.

By the end of July, Luke had cleaned all the sensors,

repaired two frayed wires, recharged the battery in the data logger, wiped dirt off the solar panel, and rebalanced the rain gauge.

"Not that you need a rain gauge right now," Dad said between bites of a grilled hot dog. He flipped through the gauge's manual. "When's the last time it rained?"

"June seventeenth," Luke answered. He braced for a taunt from his brothers, but they were too busy racing each other to see who could eat the most hot dogs.

"Sheesh, the azaleas are gonna die if it doesn't rain soon." He tossed the manual away as if it was the cause of the drought and opened another book. "Tomorrow, I want you to turn the data logger on."

"How do I start it?" Luke asked.

Dad handed him the manual and pointed to a diagram. "You connect the wires from the solar panel here. And the wires for the battery are attached here. Remember, the battery is only for backup."

"Okay."

"Woo-hoo!" Scott raised his hands into the air. "Six dogs with buns. Oh yeah, I'm the hot-dog-eating king."

"Call the *Guinness Book of World Records*," Jacob said. "Put it on speaker so I can hear them laugh at you."

"Says the man who couldn't finish five."

"I'm so proud of you both." Dad winked at Luke, including him in the joke.

Exclaiming over the time, Luke's brothers raced to get ready for their shift at the park, but Dad hung around. He cleared the table, then loaded the dishwasher. Surprised and glad for the help, Luke scrubbed the baked bean pot extra hard.

"Those two never could stay still for long." Dad slid forks into the bin. "When they were little it drove us crazy with all the noise and commotion, but when it was quiet…that meant big trouble."

"Like the time they shaved Ranger's whiskers?" Luke asked.

Dad laughed. A wonderful comforting sound Luke hadn't heard since March.

"I'd forgotten about that," Dad said.

"Or the time they built a snowman in our living room? Or the time they made a fort with the new curtains?"

"The snowman I'd never forget. I sucked water out of the carpet for days afterward." Dad filled the soap dispenser. "Good thing you were too smart to get involved with their crazy schemes."

Jacob and Scott hadn't included him in most things, but Luke didn't want to ruin this rare moment with Dad by mentioning it.

"They just don't stop to consider the circumstances," Dad said. "Unlike you. You're my thinker. I'd never trust the twins to work on Willajean's tower unsupervised, but I know you're following directions and won't hurt yourself."

Luke squared his shoulders at the compliment. *Score one for me.*

When they finished cleaning up, Dad said, "Come on, I want to show you something." He looked like a kid who had just sneaked money out of his parent's wallet.

He led Luke to the Puppy Palace. The door had been propped open to keep the shed cooler, even though the three dogs preferred to sprawl in the shade under the oak tree. Too curious to remain there, the hounds trotted over to check it out.

Luke's heart lurched. In the palace was another

bunk. On the empty wood board were a new dog's bed, a shiny stainless steel bowl, a rubber chew toy, a puppy collar, a leash, and a bag of puppy food.

"Happy belated birthday, buddy." Dad clapped him on the back. "Now we're all set for the new pup."

A shaky twirl formed in Luke's chest. As it spun, it sent off shoots of numbness that raced to Luke's hands and feet. He wanted to sink to the ground. He wanted to confess everything. All of Willajean's bloodhounds had been sold.

Instead, he picked up the thin, puppy-sized leash. "Thanks, Dad. This is great." The words tasted like rancid milk on his tongue.

"Glad you like it."

Hounddog jumped up on the new bunk and pawed at the puppy food.

"We'd better put this away." Dad shouldered the twenty-pound bag. "Open the cabinet, or Hounddog will rip the bag open and make himself sick."

When the dog food was safely inside the cabinet, Hounddog's ears drooped an inch.

Dad laughed. "Look at that face," he said. He stroked Hounddog's head. "Bloodhounds have the most expressive faces. One look, and I know exactly what they're thinking. That's why I love them."

Pins and needles flared in Luke's hands. He rubbed them and tried to relax his arms. Needing to move, Luke strode toward the house. Dad followed him into the kitchen.

"Hey, Luke," he said. "It's still early. You want to go to a movie or something?" Picking up the newspaper, Dad flipped to the entertainment section.

Luke clutched the bottom of his T-shirt. "Sure, Dad.

I just need to go to the bathroom." He bolted.

Staring into the mirror, Luke drew in a couple of deep breaths. He turned on the water and splashed a handful on his face. He stared at the faucet, then shut the water off. Reaching blindly for a towel, he pressed it to his face.

I should tell him.

Luke brushed his hair.

Why is he being so buddy-buddy now? Does he already know about the dog? Is he being nice so I'll break down and confess? No, he isn't that devious. I could tell him Willajean forgot she was giving me a bloodhound and sold them all. But what if he calls her?

Luke tossed the brush into a drawer. He hadn't been to a movie since the night Mom died. Luke wanted to replace the memory of the last movie he'd seen with a new one. Maybe then he wouldn't automatically think of Mom's death whenever someone mentioned going to the movies. With one more look in the mirror, Luke decided to talk to Dad on the drive home *after* the show.

But instead of talking about the pup, they discussed the movie.

"I can't believe he survived the fall," Dad said.

"Why not?" Luke asked. "He had his jet pack on."

"The pack had been dunked in the water. There's no way the electronics would still work after that."

"It's set in the future, Dad. I'm sure the components would be protected."

"I guess if I'm going to believe aliens invaded Earth, I can let that slide."

When they entered the house, Jacob and Scott were in the living room.

"But there's no way I'm believing that massive alien

could disguise itself as a cat." Dad tossed his keys on the table by the door. "Aliens or not, the laws of physics still apply to them."

"Why would it?" Jacob had seen the same flick the week before with Scott. "They'd have their own alien laws."

"It's call the conservation of mass and, in our universe, it's unbreakable. You can't transform a thousand-pound alien into a ten-pound house cat. If you do, where does the other 990 pounds go?" Dad asked.

"Who says the cat weighs ten pounds?" Scott asked. "Maybe he weighs a thousand."

"Can you imagine a thousand-pound cat jumping on your chest at night." Jacob laughed. "Crushed by cuteness."

"And every rat in the neighborhood would bolt," Luke said.

"Sumo Kitty, the defender of the back alley." Scott curled his fingers like claws.

Their conversation turned sillier and, laughing hard, they all tried to outdo each other by telling stories of Sumo Kitty's daring deeds. By that time, Luke wasn't about to break the family spell by mentioning the dog.

A couple of days later, Luke pedaled home fast. He skidded into the garage and dumped his bike on the floor. Racing through the house, he searched for Dad, a huge grin stretching his face. Willajean's weather station was up and running. All they had to do was calibrate the sensors, and they were good to go.

He found Dad in the Puppy Palace holding a

sledgehammer. Luke's excitement died. Fury blazed in Dad's eyes. Luke's knees locked as he jerked to a stop.

"What—?" The rest of the question stuck in Luke's throat.

Dad smashed the hammer into the new bunk he'd just built.

CHAPTER 9

Easy Peasy

Wooden splinters shot into the air as the bunk exploded. Luke jumped back, stunned by the damage.

Ranger cowered under his bunk on the opposite side of the Puppy Palace. Luke wanted to crawl under there with the dog. Dad turned to Luke, his face a mask of calm, but his tense shoulders and stiff arms warned Luke.

"Willajean called." He rested the sledgehammer on the ground.

Oh no. "Dad, I can—"

Dad put his hand up.

"She asked me if I wanted to breed Ranger to one of her bloodhounds. We discussed stud fees, and she offered first pick of the litter in lieu of money."

He opened his mouth to interrupt, but Dad shot him a warning glare. Luke had to wait for Dad to finish, or he'd be in bigger trouble.

"'Why would I need first pick?' I asked her. 'I have a new pup coming in another week.' She was quiet for so long, I thought she'd hung up on me." Dad picked up the hammer and pounded on the remaining boards still clinging to the Palace's walls. "Then she told me all the pups were sold and why."

He whacked at the wood until nothing but splinters remained. Then he rounded on Luke, "How could you lie to me and Willajean?" he demanded.

Luke had been prepared to apologize and beg for forgiveness, but Dad's questions turned his guilt into instant rage. "Lied to you?" he shouted. "I tried to talk to you. You ignored me for weeks. You only had time for me when we were working on the tower. By then it was too late." Luke grabbed the broom from the corner and started to sweep up the mess.

"I want a papillon." Luke swept the floor hard. Dust puffed around his sneakers. "I want to try a new breed." Sweep. "They're great. I was going to tell you all about them." Luke paused, huffing. "Mom thought it was a great idea, and she told me to convince you. But you won't listen to me because you blame me for her death. Don't you, Dad?" Luke stopped, shocked by his own words.

Dad gaped at him.

Hounddog and Moondoggie raced into the yard, back from their daily walk. They snuffled at the mess in the Palace. Jacob and Scott entered the shed to put the leashes away. Noticing the ruined bunk, his brothers paused.

"What happened?" Jacob asked.

"Uh…Luke…is not getting a puppy," Dad said, recovering. "Seems there was a miscommunication."

Tears pressed against the back of Luke's eyes. Dad hadn't denied hating him. Thick tension hung heavy in the air. The twins glanced at Luke with a question in their gazes.

"What Dad means is I'm not getting a bloodhound pup," Luke said with a sudden boldness. Why not? He was already deep in trouble. It couldn't get worse. Could it? "A papillon will be more comfortable in the house." Luke lifted his chin and met Dad's gaze.

"Not in *my* house," Dad dropped the sledgehammer and stalked away.

Guess it could.

"Whoa," Scott said, "Luke pissed Dad off."

"You're always screwing things up," Jacob said. "Why do you want a yappy, cotton-ball dog anyway?"

"He needs a powder puff to put on his makeup. A girly dog for a girl."

"Maybe we should buy him some dresses," Jacob said.

"Shut up!" Luke had had it with his brothers. His blood slammed through his heart. "Don't you think I feel bad enough? I get it now. You want me to suffer for causing Mom's death. I guess it makes you feel better, but nothing will bring her back."

The boys stared at him. Luke no longer cared if they beat him up; he wanted bruises and pain. He wanted another reason for the horrible burning inside him that wouldn't go away. A distraction from the all-consuming grief.

"You're crazy," Jacob said, backing away from him.

"You've been working in the hot sun too long," Scott said. "Better clean up that mess." He pointed to the remains of the bunk on the floor. "If Hounddog gets a single splinter, I'm going to pulverize you."

They retreated into the house. All of Luke's muscles shook. Jacob and Scott hadn't corrected him either. They all hated him for causing Mom's death. He gripped the broom handle to keep from sinking to the floor in a puddle of misery.

Eventually, he resumed cleaning up the mess in the Puppy Palace. The curious dogs didn't help. Whenever he bent over to use the dustpan, Hounddog thrust his nose into Luke's face. Ranger crept out from under his bunk. A sensitive and intelligent dog, Ranger would make a good father. Luke hoped that once Dad calmed down he'd consider breeding Ranger with one of Willajean's dogs.

Willajean. Dread roiled through him. How could he face her? She probably didn't want him to work for her anymore. His energy fizzled like an untied balloon zigzagging through the air.

Dragging his feet, he carried the full dustpan to the garbage can. He paused before tipping the trash inside. In a jumble at the bottom were the new dog bed and other puppy items that his father had bought him. Unable to take anymore heartache, Luke sank to the ground.

He leaned against the can, his knees pulled up to his chest, his forehead on his knees. He choked back the sobs that threatened to burst from his throat. If only Mom were here. She'd smooth things with Dad and scold his brothers. Mom would rub his back and tell him everything would be fine.

"Relax, sweetie," she'd say. "You always overthink things. Worrying about it won't change anything. Actions will. Figure out what you need to do and do it. Easy peasy."

He shook his head. Even in his imagination, Mom used one of her dumb sayings. She'd constantly embarrassed him with them. Poker straight. Snug as a bug. Cute as a button. Really? Who thought buttons were cute? Old people, he guessed.

The tightness in his chest eased a bit. Luke stood. Fishing all the new puppy supplies from the garbage can, he placed them into another bag and finished cleaning up the Palace.

At the thought of going into the house and facing Dad, Luke's heart squeezed in panic. Instead, he grabbed the bag and left. He had no destination in mind, but he ended up at the top of Willajean's driveway just as the sky darkened. Not surprising. The dogs never judged him, never got mad at him, never ignored him. Being with them gave Luke a few hours without guilt and grief – something he lacked at home.

But would he be welcome anymore? He owed Willajean an apology for lying to her. The image of Alayna's smirking face almost stopped him, but he continued to the kennel. Peeking in to visit the dogs turned out to be a bad idea. They barked as soon as they heard him, and in a matter of minutes, Willajean arrived to check out the noise.

Blunt and straight to the point as always, she said, "I talked to your father."

"I know." Luke kicked a pebble on the ground. "I'm very sorry about the papillon. But you can still sell the pup. Right?"

"I meant your father just called looking for you."

"Really?" Surprised Dad cared enough about him to call, Luke glanced at Willajean. Unless Dad wanted to yell at him or ground him or send him to foster care. Or maybe all three. His head spun. Nothing was easy peasy anymore.

She nodded. "He said you might show up here."

This is the only place I could go. Before Mom died, his best friend Ethan had invited him to the pool like he'd done every summer since they were in third grade. But Ethan hadn't talked to him since April.

Willajean watched him for a moment. "That pup's still yours. You worked hard for her."

"I can't bring her home."

She considered. "What do you have in the bag?"

"Oh, this." His face flushed with heat. Willajean probably thought he was running away from home. "Just some dog stuff. I couldn't..." Luke swallowed the rest. It was his birthday present after all, and he couldn't bear to see it thrown away.

Willajean sorted through the bag. Then she carried it over to the empty crate next to Lance's. Without asking Luke, she put the new dog bed, chew toy, and water bowl into the crate. She hung the leash and collar on the wall.

"There." Willajean stepped back. "Now your puppy has a home. She can stay as long as you need."

Luke gawked. Why wasn't Willajean mad? Was this a trick? His emotions flip-flopped between amazement, excitement, and disbelief. "But... I can't... It's too much... My dad..."

"You're still taking care of her – food, walks, clean up, training – the works. Besides, Lance is lonely out here."

"Ah…" He pressed his lips together. *Don't overthink things.* "Thanks."

Willajean smiled. "Anytime. It's getting late, I'll give you a ride home."

He followed her to her Jeep. Once inside, he rested his head back. Exhaustion swept through him. What an awful day. When she pulled up in front of his house, he panicked. "Do I have to tell my dad about the puppy?"

"What do you think?" she asked.

"That I shouldn't lie to my dad."

"Always good advice."

"But what if he tells me I can't keep her?"

"Technically, you're not keeping her, I am. But if he doesn't approve, he might not let you come over anymore."

That thought horrified him. "Then what should I do?"

"It's your decision."

Oh great. Luke slid from the car. She gave him a half-wave and drove away. He stood there on the sidewalk, watching the red tail lights fade in the distance. Maybe he should have invited her inside so Dad didn't kill him. All his muscles ached as if he'd been shoved into a giant washing machine. That about summed up his day. He was in no hurry to go inside.

He had to face Dad eventually and had to decide what to tell him.

Too bad, he had no clue.

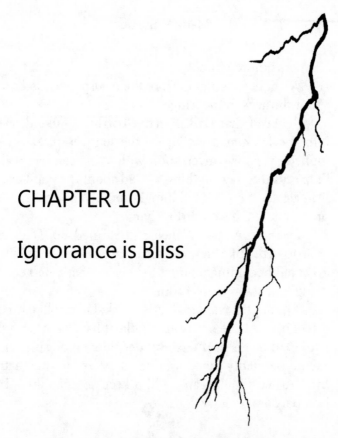

CHAPTER 10

Ignorance is Bliss

As Luke turned the knob of the front door, he braced for Dad's anger before slipping inside the house. Sitting in the recliner, Dad was reading the paper. The Phillies baseball game was on TV. Sprawled on opposite ends of the couch, Jacob and Scott tossed a soccer ball back and forth.

"They'll never make the playoffs," Scott said. "They're down ten games."

"They're a clutch team," Jacob countered. "It's only July twenty-seventh. Plenty of time for the Phils to catch up."

Luke closed the door. The lock clicked loudly. His

brothers ignored him.

Without looking up from the newspaper, Dad said, "Your dinner's in the fridge."

Relieved that Dad didn't yell at him, Luke dashed into the kitchen. Heating up the leftover pizza, Luke mulled over his conversation with Willajean. He really didn't need to say anything to Dad about the papillon. If Dad asked, then he'd tell him, if not… Why cause more problems? Luke wouldn't be lying.

By the time he finished and cleaned up, Dad had gone to bed. Luke blew out the breath he'd been holding. To avoid becoming a target for his brothers, he headed straight upstairs to his room.

Although it was only nine o'clock, Luke collapsed on top of his bed. He hoped he wouldn't have another fight with Dad or his brothers. But deep down, he suspected there'd be plenty more arguments. After all, they hated him. At least Willajean let him keep the papillon. The best part of the day.

"Willajean?" Luke gripped the phone with a sweat-slicked hand. "I can't come today. Big storm headed this way. Hurricane Boyd's supposed to take a swipe at us."

"The wind sensor is measuring wind gusts of forty miles per hour," Willajean said in amazement. "No rain yet, but I can drive you home if it does."

"No. It's too dangerous." Luke hung up the phone. Shaking, he ran into the living room to wait for the next storm update on the Weather Channel.

An insurance commercial played on the TV, quoting that more than a thousand people die each year because of the weather. Rainstorms, windstorms, snowstorms, and extreme weather like hurricanes, tornados, bitter cold, and heat waves all caused deaths. The dire statistics increased his fear.

On a nice day, learning about these storms fascinated Luke, but with a hurricane closing in, any mention of fatalities just terrified him.

It had been a beautiful summer. Until now. Luke clutched a large pillow to his pounding chest. June and July had been dry and storm free, but not August. Only ten days into the month, and the second hurricane of the season barreled toward them.

Luke hoped Willajean's tower wouldn't blow over in the storm. After the fight with Dad, Luke had figured out how to calibrate the instruments on his own. Dad was still giving him the cold shoulder.

Bitterness coated the back of Luke's throat. You're not supposed to ignore your own son. Mom would have just yelled at him, but when she calmed down, she'd hug him and apologize for losing her temper. Not Dad. He held grudges for months.

A cool graphic on the Weather Channel showed the lightning strikes within the outer rain bands of the hurricane.

Luke thought of Mom. What were the odds? Something like a million to one. Although, to be fair, the lightning had struck her van, blowing out the tires. If only she'd missed the tree...

Digging his fingers into the pillow, Luke forced his thoughts away from the accident. Was there a device that could predict where lightning would strike? If not, someone should invent a portable lightning detector for cars and for people who worked outside.

Lightning was basically electricity. How hard could

it be? The detector would need to measure the static electricity in the air. Forgetting about the impending hurricane for a moment, Luke puzzled over the problem.

Dad came into the living room and glanced at the TV. Finally, he asked, "Do you want me to ask Grandmom to come over today?"

Luke shook his head. He wouldn't risk Grandmom driving in the rain. As it was, he had to clamp his mouth shut when Dad and his brothers left for work. Previous pleas that they stay safe at home hadn't worked. Jacob and Scott had mocked him about his fear of storms since he could remember.

No one understood. Except Mom.

"It's my fault," she'd say. "I thought if you learned about what causes the thunder and lightning, you wouldn't be afraid. But it made you more scared. Now I know what they mean by *ignorance is bliss*."

The wind whistled outside. Luke checked all the windows, making sure they were secure. In the kitchen, he peered out at their fenced-in backyard. The trees creaked ominously. The Puppy Palace was under a huge oak that dropped branches during storms. With winds gusting up to seventy miles per hour, a big limb could break off and crash onto the Palace, hurting the dogs. Or killing them!

Luke clutched the counter's edge. He had to bring the dogs inside, but that meant going *outside*. Dirt and leaves blew past. The neighbor's laundry flapped. The bushes rattled. Letting go of the counter, Luke moved toward the back door. He grabbed the handle. Paused.

His heart jolted with every gust. He gauged the distance from the house to the Palace. Too far. Leaning his forehead against the door, he closed his eyes as he worked up his nerve.

I can do this. I have to do this. The dogs were part of his family. If they were hurt… *No. Not on my watch.*

In one quick motion, he straightened, yanked the door open, and bolted toward the Palace before he could change his mind. Happy to see him, the dogs circled Luke's legs and almost tripped him as they sought his attention. Sweeping his arms out, he herded them into the house. After he locked the door, he sagged against it. He'd done it.

The bloodhounds followed him into the living room – the safest spot in the house except for the basement. But Luke wouldn't go down there unless there was a tornado warning. He needed to keep an eye on the windows and the storm.

Ranger jumped onto Dad's recliner and settled down for a nap, but Hounddog and Moondoggie didn't come inside the house very often. Excited, they sniffed every inch of the carpet and explored all the rooms before plopping on the couch with Luke. After much jockeying for the best position, they draped themselves over him like a living blanket. They snored as he watched Boyd creep closer with each new radar update.

After making landfall in Delaware, Boyd lost some steam and was downgraded from a category one hurricane to a tropical storm. The outer rain bands of the still-potent storm reached central Pennsylvania by noon. Wind and rain battered the house as a shrill keening filled the air.

Thunder rumbled, vibrating deep in Luke's chest. His heart beat its own frantic storm rhythm as Boyd advanced. Despite the heat and his sweat-soaked T-shirt, Luke stayed under his dog comforter too frightened to move.

First the cable went out. Luke stared at the snowy static, willing it to come back on. Then the electricity flickered and died. Heavy rain thrummed on the roof. Tree branches twisted like acrobats in the wind.

On the edge of panic, Luke puffed for breath. The storm could destroy his house, and there was nothing Luke could do.

And yet, the dogs slept peacefully. Not a care in the world.

Ignorance really was bliss.

His brothers arrived home at six o'clock. By then, the rain had slowed to a drizzle. They'd been smart to wait until the storm had passed. But not smart enough to keep from dripping water on the carpet.

"Hersheypark closed," Jacob said. "You should see the puddles."

"Have you heard from Dad?" Luke asked. The house phone was dead, but the twins had their cells.

"Yep. He's busy with emergency calls. We won't see him for a few days."

"Why are the dogs inside?" Scott asked as Hound-dog circled his legs.

"Take a look in the back yard." Luke hooked a thumb toward the kitchen.

Curious, they went to investigate. He waited for their reactions.

"Oh crap, Dad's gonna be pissed," Jacob said.

"Maybe it's not as bad as it looks," Scott added. "Hey, Luke, come on. We'd better clean it up." He whistled for the dogs.

The three bloodhounds rushed into the kitchen, their toenails clicking on the floor. Luke hesitated, gnawing on his bottom lip. The winds had died down. Moving slowly, he joined his brothers outside. Leaves, branches, trash, and shingles covered the lawn. The dogs sniffed at the debris. The air smelled of moist earth and cut grass.

How many people had Boyd killed? Sorrow for their families pulsed in Luke's chest. At least they could blame the storm. Not that it would make them feel any better.

A big branch from the oak tree had crashed to the ground next to the Puppy Palace. Part of it had clipped the Palace's roof, damaging the front half of the shed. Luke helped his brothers move the heavy limb. The wet bark scrapped his palms and forearms.

"It's not a total loss," Scott said. "I'll get some plastic to cover the roof. Jake, why don't you find something heavy to weigh it down with. Luke, how about picking up all the broken pieces?"

They worked together. Although Luke nervously glanced at the sky from time to time, his brothers didn't tease him. Sweat stained his T-shirt, but Luke enjoyed helping Jacob and Scott. When they finished, the twins stepped back to examine their work.

"It'll do for now," Jacob said.

"Once the beds dry out, the dogs can sleep in here again." Scott looked at Luke. "Good call bringing the dogs inside."

Jacob agreed. "They could have been hurt."

Surprised at the compliment and afraid his voice would squeak, Luke nodded.

"Hey, boys," their next-door neighbor called. "Could

you help me? My umbrella blew into a tree."

"Sure thing, Mrs. Read," Scott said. "Come on, guys."

The three of them spent the rest of the evening assisting their neighbors. Despite the hard and often times muddy work, Luke had a blast.

"Today's the day," Willajean announced as she strode into the training yard. Five white puppies trotted after her.

The papillon pups were eight weeks old and ready to go to their new homes. Alayna's absence made the day extra special for Luke. Because school started next week, she'd gone shopping for school clothes.

Luke had visited the pups almost every day since they'd been born, watching and analyzing the litter. He'd like to keep them all. Each dog wore a different-colored collar. But Luke didn't need the colors to identify them. These pups were as familiar to him as the weather patterns. Each puppy had a unique personality. A distinct bark. Different markings.

The pups had been coming to the yard this past week to see what they would do. No serious training, just fun and games and treats scattered around for them to find.

The pup with the red collar headed right to Luke. Her pure white coat was unmarked along her body, but her butterfly ears and face were solid black. Grinning, Luke knelt in the grass.

"Who's a pretty girl?" He scratched behind her ears just the way she liked it.

She peered at him with quick inquisitive eyes.

Unable to resist, he picked her up, and she licked his cheek. She'd been the first pup to climb out of the whelping box, driving Willajean crazy with her escapes.

When Luke put her down, she darted quick as a whippet out to the field where the corn was as tall as Willajean. Reappearing, the dog skimmed the ground with her nose, heading straight for a treat.

"She's got the best sniffer of the pack, but she's a handful. Willful, determined, and outright stubborn. She'll either cause an ulcer or be the best tracker I've seen in awhile." Willajean rubbed her fingers on her temple.

"Do you want to keep her?" Luke asked. Athough he had first pick of the litter, he didn't want to upset Willajean. She planned to keep one of the pups.

"No way. I'm not that crazy." She grinned.

Relief filled him. "Then I'll take her."

"I thought so. Do you have a name yet?"

All the clichéd names had been rolling around his mind for the past month. Marshmallow. Sugar. White Chocolate. Angel. Nothing seemed to fit. Luke studied the puppy. Suddenly, she shot forward, beating one of her brothers to a hidden treat, then bolted past another. She was quick.

"Lightning." The name popped out of his mouth.

"Perfect. After all, she was born at Storm Watcher Kennel." Willajean's smile turned thoughtful. "I was running out of butterfly species names. Do you mind if I copy you?"

"I don't mind," Luke said, flattered. He mentally applied cool storm names to different dogs. Thunder. Blizzard. Cyclone.

Soon, Megan joined Willajean and Luke in the training yard, Lance by her side. Megan had convinced her mother to let her have him.

"You picked Red Collar, didn't you?" Megan asked.

"Yep. That obvious?"

"Oh yeah. What's her name?"

"Lightning."

"Cool! But she's going to be trouble."

"He chose the best," Willajean said. "I'm keeping Black Collar. Luke, can you name him for me?"

"Okay." *Wow, she really trusts me.*

"Thanks." Willajean, her expression sad, petted Lance.

Luke wondered how he'd feel if six months from now he had to give Lightning up. Awful. Sick to his stomach. Lousy.

Did Megan notice her mom's grief? He glanced at Megan, but she was watching the pups. Did she know Willajean was a great mom to let her train Lance? Or would she only realize it later? Like him. He remembered the time Mom bought him a Hershey Bears sweatshirt with her teapot money. She'd been saving for a laptop.

"I can wait a few more weeks," Mom had said, waving it off.

He'd thanked her, but now he understood she never would have gotten that laptop. Every time Luke or his brothers wanted something that they didn't need, Mom dipped into her teapot and bought it.

If only he could have one more day with Mom. Just one day to tell her how much she meant to him and to apologize.

I was safe inside the move theater. I shouldn't have called her to come get me.

Swallowing, Luke focused on the present. Willajean and Megan had moved away as if they sensed he needed some space. Odd how he could be having a great day, and then…*wham*! A memory or guilt would ruin it.

Okay that's enough. He concentrated on the puppies. The black-collared pup was a chubby male. He liked to barrel through his littermates, using his weight to push them aside.

Luke smiled as the perfect name came to him. "Hurricane."

During the afternoon, families arrived to pick up their new puppies. After each pup left, Willajean disappeared into the house and only returned when the next car drove down the driveway.

Willajean greeted the last customer with a red nose and blotchy skin.

"Is your mom sick?" Luke asked Megan.

"No. Mom's upset to see the puppies go. I'm not. They almost destroyed the sunroom last night, and I'm tired of cleaning up after them."

Luke understood both of them. He'd miss them all, but a part of him agreed with Megan. The litter had been a handful, and now he could concentrate all his attention on Lightning.

After the last customer left, Willajean moved Lightning and Hurricane into the big crate next to Lance so they wouldn't be lonely.

As they prepared the food for the next day, another car crunched along the drive. Willajean hurried out. Soon voices approached the kennel. Luke and Megan exchanged a concerned look when Willajean entered with a scowling man.

"I'm sorry about the mix-up, Rodney. I had you

down for one of Sweetie's pups. You can have the puppy I saved for myself." Willajean picked up Hurricane. "He's a—"

"I don't want a male. I *specifically* requested a female so I can breed her. The creases in Rodney's face deepened.

Oh no. Luke clutched his hands together. Willajean had promised this man a papillon, and the only female left was Lightning. His good mood fled in an instant.

"I'm really sorry. You can have pick of my next litter. Sweetie—"

"I want a pup from Lady. She has excellent markings." Rodney stabbed a finger at Lightning. "What about this one? Is it a female?"

A numb horror washed over Luke. No way Willajean would upset a paying customer.

"She's sold to someone else." Willajean kept her gaze on Rodney.

"Can you see if your other customer will wait for a pup from Sweetie? I paid top dollar for this dog, and I've a timeline of my own, you know."

A painful knot gripped Luke's stomach. The last thing he wanted was to lose Lightning, but Willajean had been so nice to him, and she'd done so much for him. She needed his help this time. He couldn't be selfish.

Could he?

CHAPTER 11

The Boy Whose Mother Died

"Take her," Luke said to Rodney. "I can wait for the next litter." His heart shattered.

"No," Willajean said. "I've first pick of Robert Crick's litter." Before Rodney could protest, she held up a hand. "The stud's the same one I used for Lady, and the mother is Crimson Ivy of Hundred Acre Kennels. You can have that pup. The litter will be ready next week."

Luke gaped at Willajean. He opened his mouth to object, but the words caught in his throat.

"Crimson Ivy? She won best in breed at Westminster." Rodney's face smoothed, and his blue eyes glowed. "Are you sure?"

"Quite certain. Do we have a deal?"

"Of course." Rodney pumped Willajean's hand. With a smile and wave he left the kennel.

"But, Willajean…" Completely at a loss, Luke spread his hands.

"Lightning is your puppy. I promised you first. Besides, I made the mistake. You shouldn't suffer because of it."

Yeah, but people suffered all the time over other people's mistakes. His dad and brothers hurt because of him. And his mom—

Willajean returned Hurricane to the crate and headed for the house. Luke let Lightning out. He gave the little dog a quick hug.

"Wow, Luke, that was really really nice," Megan said.

He shrugged. "You'd do the same, right?"

"Wrong. I wouldn't give up Lance for all the money in the world."

He kept quiet. She didn't understand why he'd offered Lightning to the man. It was like Mom's teapot money. She could have spent it on herself, but she didn't. Mom enjoyed spending it on her sons. To Luke, seeing Willajean happy was more important.

Megan and Luke resumed preparing the dogs' food in the kitchen while Lance and Lightning dove for anything that dropped on the floor.

"I don't want to go to school," Megan said as she peeled the carrots. "Alayna's all excited. She even has her first day outfit ironed and hanging in her closet. She'll love being the new girl and getting all the attention. I won't."

"It's better than being ignored," Luke said, thinking of his friend, Ethan, who'd avoided him after Mom died.

Plus Dad still evaded him with the determination of an army drill sergeant.

"No it isn't. I'd rather no one noticed me. I'd rather be going to my school back in North Carolina."

"You can text your friends at lunch." Luke dumped rice into the cooker.

"Really? They let you text in school?"

"Only at lunch."

"That's pretty cool."

"I guess. But if you're caught texting at any other time, your cell phone is confiscated. And the only way to get it back is for one of your parents to pick it up." He added water and turned the cooker on.

"That probably won't happen to me. I don't get many texts anymore," Megan said in a quiet voice.

Luke glanced at her. She was chopping the onions with extra force. Were those tears on her cheeks from the onions or not? He kinda understood how she felt. Megan had moved away from her friends, but Luke's had backed away from him.

Partly my fault. Being around Ethan – who still had his mother – hurt too much. The few times he'd gotten together with his friend after the accident had been complete disasters. But now… Now he could handle it better, but it was too late.

"I'd text you if I had a phone," Luke said.

"So you can tell me how great Lightning is?" She smirked at him.

"Of course. Did I tell you she almost caught a cricket this morning?"

Megan rolled her eyes. "Many times."

They pulled the frozen meat from the freezer.

"I'm going to miss Lighting when we go back to

school," Luke said.

"She's so small, you can probably smuggle her into class in your backpack." Megan laughed.

Luke didn't. Megan's comment had struck him like lightning.

No storms threatened for the first day of school. A good sign. Luke pedaled to Willajean's. Today was one of the few days Luke didn't mind going to school. Everything would be new – teachers, classes, locker, schedule. But soon it would fade into boredom and routine.

At least this year he had Lightning.

He arrived at the kennel in time to help finish the morning feeding. Alayna wore an apron so her new clothes wouldn't get dirty. Megan pretended to spill a bowl of dog food on her sister. Alayna shrieked and complained to Willajean, who ignored her.

After the last dog was fed, Luke had a few minutes to play with Lightning before they needed to leave.

"Hey, Luke, can you check the temperature sensor after school?" Willajean asked.

"Sure. Why?"

"I think one of the wires is loose. I looked at the data Alayna recorded yesterday, and it reported a high temperature of twenty degrees."

"Does she know how to work the data logger?" he asked.

Alayna glared at him. "If you can do it, any idiot can do it too."

"So you're an idiot then?" Megan asked.

Alayna rounded on Megan, who smiled sweetly at

her.

"I don't have time to bother with *children*." Alayna slammed the door behind her and headed up the driveway.

"There goes the princess." Megan pretended to bow. "Going to catch her big yellow carriage."

Luke laughed. "We'd better get going, too."

Megan kicked off her work boots and put on a pair of flip-flops. She wore jean shorts and a T-shirt like always, but these didn't have any stains or holes in them. Her messenger bag was clean, too. Luke fingered the duct tape on his shoulder strap. He had fixed Jacob's old backpack because his was beyond repair.

As they biked to school, she stayed right next to him. Luke did all the talking.

"You'll like Mr. Savoca, he never gives homework."

"Don't eat the taco salad unless you want to burp all day."

"Don't use the water fountain next to the gym. The water tastes like metal, and it's warm. There's another one right around the corner that's newer."

"Avoid Mr. Adams, the athletic director. He's tall and bald, so you can't miss him. If you catch his attention, he'll bug you to sign up for a sport."

Megan locked her bike next to Luke's but hung back as he headed for the front doors. She was acting weird. He'd bet if the school had been full of dogs, she'd be running inside. Thinking about it, he guessed he'd act the same way if this was his first day in a brand-new school.

"Come on," he said. "I'll show you around."

He led her through the crowded and noisy hallways. Kids stared at them both. A new kid walking with the boy whose mother died. A strange pair. Luke kept moving, ignoring the gawkers. Nothing could help him, but Megan needed a friend who wouldn't attract as much attention. He scanned lockers and spotted Jenna.

Jenna was nice to everyone. She was also a math genius and had helped him a couple times last year without making him feel stupid. Plus she didn't get as awkward after his Mom died. She'd treated him almost the same. He slowed. Would she still be okay?

"Uh, Jenna…"

"Hey, Luke. How was your summer?" Jenna smiled.

"Uh, fine. This is Megan, she's new and—"

"Hi, Megan. Where are you from?"

"North Carolina," Megan said.

After that, it didn't take Jenna long to drill Megan about her schedule. Megan handed Jenna her class list in self-defense.

"Oh, my God, we have fourth period geometry and first period earth science together," Jenna said. She tugged on Megan's arm. "The science lab is down this hallway. Let's go. Later, Luke."

Megan flashed him a big grin as she followed Jenna. He shot her a thumbs-up before reporting to his first period class. English. *Ugh*. His least favorite subject. And to make it worse, Ethan sat three seats away. He didn't glance up as Luke passed him. A complete dodge.

Luke hunched over his desk and fidgeted with his pencil. And tried not to stare at the tall, thin boy that had once been his best friend. Ethan's hair had turned almost white from the sun, and his tanned skin meant he'd had spent his summer at the pool. Luke wondered who Ethan had invited to go with him this year. Matt or Grant? Both? Luke's stomach churned.

The day went downhill from there. Just like at the end of last year, kids whispered behind his back. The teachers treated him as if he'd break. After a summer with Megan, he'd forgotten how weird everyone had been around the boy whose mother died.

By the time he met Megan at the bike rack after school, he wanted to scream. Instead, he pedaled fast, heading toward the kennel. He had to get far away or he'd burst. Megan did all the talking.

"Jenna is super sweet. She already texted me at lunch."

"The brownies were unbelievable. At my old school all we had for dessert was pudding."

"Did you know earth science has a meteorology unit? I bet you'll ace that test."

"We got brand-new textbooks in history. I love the smell of new books."

When they reached the kennel, Luke dumped his bike and ran inside. Lightning yipped, dancing with excitement. He picked her up. She licked his nose. And he no longer wanted to scream.

Every morning, Luke biked to Willajean's and met up with Megan. After school they raced back to the kennel to play with their dogs, help with the late afternoon training session, and record weather data for Willajean.

He stayed at Willajean's as long as possible, doing homework with Megan and eating dinner with her family a couple times a week. Dad didn't seem to mind that Luke was never home. At least, he hadn't said anything. But Luke and Dad weren't exactly talking.

They exchanged a few words before both bolting, and Luke spent a ton of time in his room alone. This awkward relationship had a good side – no conversations about the puppy or school, and a bad – Dad still hated him. Luke's insides knotted.

By mid-October Lightning was housebroken and had learned a few good manners like sit, stay, and be quiet when signaled. All Luke had to do was place his finger on his lips, and she'd settle down.

On the morning of the seventeenth, the Weather Channel tracked a Nor'easter brewing close to the East Coast and heading north. Heavy rain was predicted for central Pennsylvania on the eighteenth. Luke would miss school tomorrow.

After the afternoon training session was completed, Luke pulled a couple of his books from his backpack and hid them in the kennel. Then he put Lightning into his backpack.

He left the top unzipped, and Lightning stood on the remaining books, poking her head through the gap. Not sure what she would do, Luke mounted his bike and started out slowly. The little dog stayed in the pack and seemed to enjoy the wind in her face.

When he reached home, he pulled off his pack, gave Lightning the quiet signal, and pushed her down so he could zip it closed. Dad barely glanced up as Luke hurried upstairs to his room. And for once, Luke's chest didn't tighten over being ignored. He let Lightning out, pressing a finger to his lips again. She sniffed every inch of the room before settling down on the bed.

Happy for the first time since March, Luke curled up next to her. Before turning out the light, he called

Megan. "Just so you know, I brought Lightning home."

Surprised, Megan asked, "Your dad let you?"

"No. I snuck her in."

"What about tomorrow morning? Won't your dad see her when you leave for school?"

"I'm not going to school. Dad will cover for me," Luke explained. Dad let him stay home on stormy days.

"Luke, what's with you and the rain?" Megan asked. "My mom can drive us."

He bit his lip. Should he tell Megan and risk having her laugh at him?

"I don't like it," he said quietly into the phone.

"Like what?"

"Being exposed. Being at the mercy of the forces of nature. Forces that don't care if they ruin your life."

"Oh," Megan said. "Is this about…your mom?"

"You know?" If Megan started treating him different, he'd… *What*? Not much he could do. It would just suck big time.

"We knew she'd…died, but not how or when. Jenna told me the details."

Great. The silence on the phone stretched past awkward. "I never liked storms. Even when I was little. What happened to my mom just proves how dangerous they are."

Another pause. *Oh no, here comes some stupid comment about Mom being in heaven, or it was just her time.* Words that made it hurt more.

"Guess it sucked being right," Megan said.

"Yep."

"Want me to get your assignments tomorrow?"

"No," he said quickly. He didn't want Megan to make a special trip in the rain just for him. If Luke had his way, all his family and friends would stay home during storms. Too bad, he never got his way.

At least he had Lightning to keep him company this time. The next morning after everyone left, Luke let Lightning out of his room. She explored every corner before curling up on his lap while he watched the Weather Channel. Luke gazed at the small dog and wished Mom could have met her. He smiled just imagining it.

Mom would have been all obnoxious. "Told you she'd be perfect, Luke. Didn't I?"

He'd agree, and then she'd coo over Lightning and feed her treats, spoiling the dog rotten. Just like she'd done with the bloods. They'd all lost weight since March. Luke wondered if they missed her, too. Funny that he'd never thought about it before now.

"Do you have big plans for tomorrow?" Megan asked. She was playing tug-of-war with Lance. When she won, she threw the toy. Lance and Lightning chased after it.

The dogs loved the cold. They tore around the training yard full of energy. Luke pushed his hands deeper into the pockets of his jacket as he shivered, thinking of the warm kennel and hot food. It would be dark soon.

"We're going to my grandmom's for dinner," he said.

So far, Luke's first Christmas without Mom was a horror best forgotten. No decorations, no parties, and no presents from Dad under the tree. Dad had been working overtime since early November, so they'd skipped Thanksgiving this year. And Luke suspected

Dad would work tomorrow as well. A furnace would burn out, and Dad would rush off so *strangers* could have a warm Christmas. At least Grandmom had promised a special Italian dinner of homemade pasta and tomato sauce.

"Are you guys doing anything?" he asked.

"Not really. We used to visit Poppy every Christmas, but now it's just us." Megan grabbed the end of the toy hanging from Lance's mouth. "Alayna and I wanted to go to North Carolina and visit our friends, but Mom said maybe in the spring." Grunting, she yanked the toy from Lance and tossed it hard. "By spring we'll be breeding the dogs."

"At least we don't have school." Eleven days to spend with Lightning. And with Dad so busy, Luke could sneak her home. Maybe he could bring her to Grandmom's house.

Tires crunched on gravel. An old, dented Ford Ranger turned down the driveway.

"Oh no." Megan stared at the pickup truck in horror.

"What's wrong?"

The truck drove up to the house, and a man stepped out.

"Oh no. Oh no. Oh no." Megan pressed her hands to her face.

"What?"

She turned. "Quick. Put the dogs inside and lock the doors."

"Why?"

"My dad's here."

CHAPTER 12

Electric Potato

"Your dad?" Luke scooped Lightning into his arms and held her close. "Should we call the police?"

Megan scowled. "No. The police in North Carolina said he hadn't done anything illegal. They said he owned the puppies, and it was a domestic dispute." Megan called Lance.

They whistled for the dogs and hurried them into the kennel.

"But what about the other puppies he stole?" Luke asked in panic. He wished the dog crates had locks.

"No evidence."

Luke glanced at the crate with Hurricane. If he disappeared, Luke'd be sick. "Should I take him home with me?"

"No. I'll lock the door to the kennel. My dad won't have a key." She peered out the window. "Besides, Mom has a twelve-gauge shotgun, so he'll be leaving very soon."

Glad Willajean could handle the situation, Luke relaxed. They waited, but nothing happened. Eventually, Megan's phone vibrated with a text from Alayna ordering her home.

Luke and Megan looked at each other.

"What do you think that means?" Luke asked.

"I don't know."

"Do you want me to come with you?"

"No. You'd better go. I'll call you later."

Luke pounced on the phone after the first ring. "Hello?"

"She's letting him stay," Megan's voice shrilled.

"What?" Not what he'd expected. Worry flared up.

"He conned her. Told her he's been in rehab these last four months and is now clean and sober. He promised he'd pay her back for the puppies. His coming here to make amends is part of his recovery or something like that." Megan sighed. "And it's Christmas Eve. Mom said we should give him a chance to prove he's changed. He's gonna stay in the apartment in the barn for a few days."

"There's an apartment in there?" He'd thought they only used it for storage now that the cows were gone.

"Yeah. Poppy use to rent it out. He liked the company. Mom's been fixing it up. It's not done, but it's livable." She didn't sound at all happy about it.

Luke understood her concern. "What about the dogs?"

"Don't worry, I'm gonna make sure they don't disappear."

"How?"

"I'll sleep in the kennel."

"Will your mom let you?" he asked.

"I'm not asking her."

"What if she finds out?"

"She won't. I'm always up first in the morning. And it's only for a few days."

Except a few days turned into a few weeks as her father supposedly searched for a job.

"Can I come over?" Megan asked.

Since her father had returned, Megan had been hanging out at Luke's house whenever possible. They still worked at the kennel and collected weather data right after school, but as soon as dinner was over, Megan bolted.

"I'm training Lance to be an air-scenting dog," Megan told Dad one night as she helped him put the dishes away.

While Luke wrote down homework problems at the kitchen table, Megan and Dad discussed the pros and cons of air-scent versus ground-scent. Luke sighed. Megan treated Dad like a celebrity, following him around the house like a groupie.

"Hey, Megan. We have to finish the geometry assignment." Luke tried to keep the annoyance out of his voice.

She plopped down in a seat and made an attempt at her homework. As soon as Dad left the kitchen, she said, "Your dad is so great. He knows so much about search and rescue. My father's such a weasel."

"He's okay. What answer did you get for problem two?"

They solved proofs until Jacob and Scott burst into the kitchen.

"We came to check on the lovebirds," Jacob said.

"Puppy love is so cute," Scott said. "I bet their hands accidentally touch while they picked up poop. Love at first scoop."

Luke ignored them, but he worried about Megan. She was fresh blood, and she had been coming long enough to no longer be considered a guest. In other words, fair game.

Megan's brown eyebrows pinched together in thoughtful confusion. "How old are you?" she asked Scott.

"We'll be seventeen in May. Why?" Scott asked.

Luke had to fight to keep from smiling. It was the middle of January.

"Juniors, right?" she asked.

They nodded.

"You have jobs. Drive a car. You're both training to be SAR volunteers. Right?"

Jacob and Scott exchanged puzzled looks.

"I was just making sure," Megan said. "You're acting like a couple of fourth graders. I thought I was wrong about your age."

They stammered.

"Maybe you're just mentally delayed." She tapped a finger on her lip as if considering.

They didn't wait around to hear the prognoses.

"Awesome." Luke high-fived Megan across the table.

She laughed. Both in a good mood despite having to do proofs, they finished their homework. When Megan heard her dad's voice in the living room, her smile disappeared. Without another word, she packed her books.

Luke had only met Megan's dad a couple of times. Mr. Duncan had the same dark hair and eyebrows as Megan, but his fashion sense matched Alayna's. He dressed like one of those clothes models in the glossy flyers in the Sunday paper. According to Megan, Alayna had been thrilled by their dad's arrival.

Megan's dad acted nice. If Luke hadn't known about the stolen puppies, he probably would have been taken in. As it was, Luke felt uneasy in the man's presence.

"Come on, Meggie. Time to go," Mr. Duncan called.

Luke and Megan entered the living room.

"I still can't figure out why the electricity doesn't work," Mr. Duncan said to Dad. "I'm sick of using the wood stove and kerosene lamps. Can you stop over sometime and help me?" He glanced around the room. "I'll pay, of course. You could probably use the money."

And where would Mr. Duncan get the money? By stealing more puppies? Luke waited for his father to explode.

Instead Dad said, "I'll give you a call," in that flat, dangerous tone.

Megan's father had no clue. "Great. I'm sure we'll figure it out." He waved good-bye and ushered Megan through the door.

In the silence that followed their departure, Luke searched Dad's face.

"Idiot." Dad shook his head.

"You're not calling," Luke said.

"You got that right."

Due to an especially snowy January, Luke missed a number of school days. He started bringing Lightning home every night and then returning her to Willajean's before school. To avoid getting caught, Luke let Lightning outside for a bathroom break after Dad went to bed. In the morning, he waited until Dad had left for work.

One night in mid-January, Lightning woke Luke from a sound sleep. She whined and pawed at his arm. The clock read 2:20 a.m.

Groggy, he blinked at her for a moment. "Go back to sleep," he whispered, giving her the quiet signal.

She jumped off the bed and stood next to the door. Her impatient jiggling cut right through his sleep fog. Lightning needed to go out. Now.

Groaning, Luke rolled from bed, then picked her up. He crept downstairs because Dad's bedroom was next to the stairs. He let her down, grabbed his coat, and shoved his bare feet into his cold and still damp snow boots. *Ugh*.

A blast of icy air hit Luke as he opened the door. Lightning dashed through his legs and into the snow-covered yard. Luke flipped on the back porch light. Snowflakes swirled in the beam of light. Pulling his coat around his shoulders, Luke stood on the porch, waiting for her. He hoped Hounddog and Moondoggie wouldn't bark.

"What are you doing out here?" Dad asked.

Luke jumped. "Ah! You scared me." His heart slammed in his chest.

"Sorry." Dad waited.

He thought fast. "I'm...um checking the snowfall." He gestured to the ruler he had buried in the snow during a previous storm. "Seeing if there's enough snow for school to be canceled tomorrow."

"And you had to do this now?"

"Yeah. I...uh couldn't sleep." Luke kept his gaze on Dad, but silently willed Lightning to stay away.

"Well?"

"Oh. Only a couple inches so far, but we might get more by morning."

"Come inside, it's freezing." Dad shooed Luke into the house. He closed and locked the door. "Go back to bed."

"Uh, I'm going to heat up a glass of milk. Maybe that'll help me sleep."

Dad gave him a long look. Unable to keep still, Luke broke eye contact. He hung up his coat, filled a glass with milk, and put it into the microwave. Guilt over lying to Dad warred with fear. And a part of Luke wanted to get it over with so he could have it out with his father. They hadn't spoken much since the whole dog fiasco. So Luke didn't know where he stood with Dad. *Does he still hate me?*

Dad finally said, "Don't be up too late."

"Okay. Goodnight."

"Night."

Luke waited until Dad's bedroom door clicked shut before checking on Lightning. She sat on the porch. Snowflakes clung to her long hair. He let her in and dried her off before taking her and the warm milk up to his room.

Unable to sleep, Luke stared at the ceiling, his chest tight with an uneasy feeling. He should 'fess up about Lightning. Except Dad wouldn't let her stay, and Luke wouldn't be able to face his empty room. He'd have to sleep in the kennel with Megan.

Megan still avoided her dad. But Mr. Duncan kept trying to spend time with her. Unlike his dad. Luke guessed he'd have to make the first move. Too bad he had no idea how to do it.

"Have you decided what you're going to do?" Megan leaned against the locker next to Luke's.

"No." Luke pulled out his science textbook. "But we have until February first to pick a topic."

"That's tomorrow."

Oh no. "I've got nothing. You took the best idea." He slammed the locker door shut.

"You can't use it. It's against the rules."

"I know." Everyone knew Dad did search and rescue so Luke had to find a science fair project that didn't copy one of his dad's professions. Parents were allowed to help, but they couldn't be experts.

Megan frowned. "Then why are you mad at me?"

Because he needed an excuse to hang out with his dad. But he couldn't say that to Megan.

"Sorry." He zipped his backpack. "Are you going to bring Lance to school for the science fair?"

Mentioning dogs always made her smile. It worked.

"If I'm allowed. I'm gonna make a poster on how to train a SAR dog, then have a few of the tools needed on display, and to top it off, I'll demonstrate the technique to the judges with Lance."

"Isn't it risky to use Lance? He might slobber all over the judges," he teased.

"You're just jealous 'cause there's a blue ribbon in my future."

"No way. My electric potato is gonna rock the house."

She laughed. "I hope you come up with a better idea than *that.*"

He hoped so, too.

"Think of what you're good at, Luke."

"That won't take long."

She swatted his arm. "You're good at math."

"Jenna's better."

"Okay, I give up. Have fun with your potato."

CHAPTER 13

Spare Parts

In a panic, Luke read through the science fair rules again that night. The instructions suggested project ideas, but nothing interested him. Finally, he made a list of his skills. Math, science, and dogs. He'd gotten pretty good at training the papillon puppies in tracking. But Megan's project was too close.

He tried another tactic. What would he want to do when he grew up? He'd like to own a kennel like Willajean's someday. Own a farm with cows, sheep, and chickens. He'd install a big Doppler radar system instead of a little weather tower.

The weather tower. Excitement built inside him. They'd been collecting data since he fixed it. Maybe he could use the data to... What? He'd need years worth of data to predict weather trends. He could compare her tower's readings with the National Weather Service's data, but what would that prove?

Another idea hit him. He dashed downstairs to get the instrument manuals he still hadn't returned to Willajean. Maybe he could make his own instruments and compare them to Willajean's tower. *How hard could it be?*

Sitting at the kitchen table, Luke read through the wind speed manual. Building one would be difficult. Unless…

Luke grabbed the manuals and went out to the living room. Dad sat at the desk, paying bills.

"Uh…Dad."

"Yeah?" He typed a few numbers on the calculator.

"I thought of a science fair project."

"Uh-huh. That's great." Dad ripped a check off and stuck it into an envelope.

Luke crushed the manuals to his chest. "I'm gonna build an electric potato."

"What?" He glanced at Luke, scrunching up his nose so his reading glasses wouldn't slide off.

Now that Luke had Dad's full attention, he explained his idea about building weather instruments. "Can you help me?"

"Sure, buddy. It'll be fun." Dad smiled at him.

With that smile, some of the tension between them melted. But happy and guilty emotions mixed. Dad didn't know Lightning was upstairs sleeping on Luke's bed.

The next day Dad brought a bag full of electrical

supplies home for their weather station. After dinner they rummaged in the basement for more supplies. Luke decided to focus on building wind speed and direction sensors.

They dumped their odd collection of gadgets onto the kitchen table.

"Now we need a design," Dad said.

"We can copy the instruments on Willajean's tower." Luke suggested.

"We could, but that would be boring."

Luke glanced up in surprise.

"Think about it. Both sensors spin and use magnets to create an electrical current. Maybe we can combine them into one instrument," Dad said.

Luke considered. They'd need something that spun with the force of the wind, but that would also rotate to point out the direction of the wind. "An airplane," Luke cried. "With the propeller measuring wind speed, and the body of the plane pointing to the wind direction."

"Good idea. You have a head for engineering. Not like your brothers, who think an ohm meter is used for measuring the thickness of hair gel."

Smiling, Luke sat a little straighter. Maybe Dad would teach him more about electricity. That would be cool.

They worked on their weather instruments every night for the rest of the week.

"We don't have a fancy computer processor," Dad said when Luke wondered how they would record weather data. "We'll have to make do with some old-fashioned equipment."

"Such as?"

"You tell me. It's your project."

Luke thought about it. Wind direction was basically a compass point so a metal circle underneath with the directions marked should work. He etched in the sixteen compass points so he would be able to record the direction. As for wind speed... He tapped his pencil on his lips. An ohm meter had a spinning magnet generating an electrical current so it should be able to measure wind speed. Luke could then calculate how fast the wind was by the strength of the current. Faster wind equaled more electricity.

On Saturday morning, Luke and Dad connected their homemade instruments onto Willajean's tower. Lance, Lightning, and Hurricane had trotted after them. They played in the snow, while Luke and Dad worked.

After they finished, Dad watched the pups. Lance looked out of place with his darker coat and long legs.

"They're cute little fuzz balls," Dad said.

Luke quickly added, "And smart, too." He called them over and told them to sit, go down, and roll over. All three obeyed.

Dad's gaze returned to the weather tower.

Nothing special about those tricks. Time for some fun. Luke pointed to his nose. The dogs stared at him with their undivided attention.

"Tag," he said. "Lance is it."

Lance surged to his feet and chased the other two. When he butted Hurricane with his nose, Luke called, "Hurricane's it."

Hurricane spun and took off after Lightning. The dogs played tagged with Luke's help. Lightning was never it for long. She could even catch Lance. Luke beamed at her. When he stopped the exercise, Luke had Dad's interest.

"Impressive. Did Willajean train them?"

"No. Megan and I have been working with them. We're going to teach them hide-and-go-seek next."

"Clever names. They match the kennel."

"Thanks," Luke said.

Dad glanced at him, waiting.

"Willajean let me name them." He drew in a deep breath and took a big risk. "Lightning's my dog," he blurted.

Luke braced for his dad's anger, but Dad's expression didn't change.

"It's getting cold, we'd better head back. Make sure you get out here as much as possible. The more data you record, the better your results will be."

Annoyed that Did didn't acknowledge his comment about Lightning, Luke said gruffly, "I know. Willajean and Megan offered to record data, too."

"Good." Dad ignored Luke's attitude.

Luke tapped his chest. Lightning jumped into his arms, and he carried her. The dog's warmth soaked right through his winter coat.

When they returned the dogs, Dad talked to Willajean and toured the kennel. Luke joined Megan in the kitchen.

"What did he say about Lightning?" Megan asked.

"Nothing."

"Ah, too bad."

"I'm not so sure. My dad's hard to read." Luke played with the zipper on his coat. "Maybe if he sees me with Lightning and sees how smart she is, he'll come around."

"As long as he doesn't see you with her at *your* house."

"I guess." He remembered the night he almost got

caught. Did Dad already suspect Lightning came home with him at night?

Dad's voice sounded around the corner. "You have a nice place here, and Luke's learned a lot about training dogs."

"He's easy to teach, the kid's a sponge," Willajean said.

Luke puffed up his chest, smirking at Megan.

Megan snorted. "You're more like a barnacle."

Willajean and Dad entered the kennel kitchen, and Dad glanced around in surprise. He admired the full-sized freezer. "I've always wanted one of these."

A door slammed, and they all peered out the window. Mr. Duncan strode toward the kennel. Megan groaned, and Willajean frowned at her.

Dad checked his watch. "I'd better go, or I'll be late for training."

"Can I come with you?" Megan asked in a rush. "Since I'll be training Lance for SAR, it'll be good for me to observe. And it'll help with my science fair project too."

Luke held his breath. Dad didn't let Scott and Jacob go along until they were fifteen.

"If it's okay with your mom." Dad pulled out his keys.

"What about your chores?" Willajean asked her.

"Luke can finish them for me. Right, Luke?"

Still surprised by Dad's response, Luke blinked. Megan's gaze pleaded with him.

"Sure."

"All right, but remember your manners and don't be a pest, asking a million questions," Willajean said.

The kitchen door swung open. Dad and Megan dashed out, leaving Luke and Willajean without saying good-bye.

"Hey, where are you going?" Mr. Duncan called after them.

No answer. They were too busy escaping.

For the science fair, Luke collected four weeks of wind data to compare to Willajean's instruments. He made a colorful poster display using pictures of the tower and the instruments in various stages of completion. Setting up his project in the cafeteria, he mounted his airplane sensor on a wooden stand between the poster and a bar graph of the results. His wind sensor had performed well. Not perfect, but within a compass point for the wind direction, and within five miles per hour for the wind speed. Not bad for spare parts.

Megan set up across from him, but he avoided talking to her. Angry about not being able to bring Lance to school, she complained about it to everyone who stopped by her station.

When it was time to declare the winners of the science fair, Luke's stomach turned inside out. Dad stood next to him. His father hadn't attended any school programs since Mom died almost a year ago.

The loud speaker whined and popped as the principal's voice boomed over the cafeteria. Luke barely heard the standard congratulations to all who had participated...*blah, blah, blah*. Nervous energy tingled on his skin, and if the principal didn't hurry up, he'd explode.

"And now to announce the winners..."

CHAPTER 14

One in a Million

Luke stopped breathing.

Principal Weaver cleared his throat. "Third place goes to...Emily Greenly for her in-depth analysis of stink bugs."

Applause filled the room. When the noise died down, the principal said, "Congratulations Emily, I'm sure we'll all be using that information to get rid of those stinky devils in the fall."

Laughter. Luke's heart banged against his rib cage. *Come on.*

"Second place goes to..." A pause as the sound of rustling papers echoed from the speakers.

"Luke Riley for his wind analysis and weather

instruments."

Luke was so shocked, all his breath whooshed out in one gasp. More applause sounded, his brothers whooped, and Dad pulled Luke into a bear hug. The rest of the announcements garbled together. Later, he learned Megan earned an honorable mention, and Grant Brubaker won first place with his mini-bot.

Megan scowled.

"Honorable mention is great," Luke said. "You beat out Ben Good's flea circus. He's been bragging about that sketchy project for weeks."

"Yeah, it's okay," she said, but her gaze was on her father. "What's he doing here? He never comes to these things."

Luke didn't answer. Another honorable mention ribbon caught his eye. Ethan held it up, smiling for a picture. His mom snapped a bunch. Luke remembered she'd always taken pictures of everything. Their house was covered with photos. He waited for the sharp stab of jealousy and throat-closing misery, but only an ache of sadness throbbed. Maybe it wasn't too late. Maybe Ethan had been waiting for him to make the first move.

Making a sudden decision, Luke strode over to Ethan. "Hey, congrats on the honorable mention."

"Uh, thanks. You too." Ethan gestured to Luke's red ribbon.

"Thanks. Um…my brothers bought a whole box of old video games at a garage sale, and some of them are pretty cool. Want to come over on Saturday and check them out?" Luke tried to sound casual like it would be no big deal if Ethan said no.

"Uh…" Ethan glanced at his mom. "Can I?"

She checked her phone. "You have a dentist

appointment in the morning. How about in the afternoon?"

"That's fine. See you." Luke hustled back to Dad and his brothers.

After the fair, they celebrated Luke's second place with ice cream. Banana splits for the whole family.

Mom's favorite.

Ethan's mom dropped him at Luke's house on Saturday afternoon. Luke opened the door.

"Text me when you're ready to come home," his mom called through the car window.

"Okay."

"Do you have your phone?"

"Yes." Ethan waved her away, then stepped inside.

For an awkward moment, they both stood there not sure what to say or do. The last time they'd hung out, Luke had yelled at Ethan, calling him a jerk. And now he couldn't even remember why they'd gotten into the fight.

Luke closed the door. "You got a phone?"

Ethan pulled a smart phone from his pocket and handed it to him. "Yep, for my thirteenth."

"Sweet." Luke scrolled through the apps. "Too bad we don't have wi-fi."

"Seriously? Dude, you need to get into the twenty-first century."

"Tell that to my dad. I don't have a phone yet either."

"Isn't that considered neglect? Even sixth graders have phones."

Oh, great. Luke handed the phone back.

"You could ask for one for your birthday." Ethan glanced around as if remembering something. "Weren't you supposed to get a pup for your thirteenth?"

"I did."

"Where is he? In the Palace with the other mutts?"

Luke smiled. His brothers would pound Ethan if they'd heard that. "No. She's at Storm Watcher Kennel."

"Where? Why?"

Luke headed into the living room. "It's messed up."

"Couldn't be worse than living in four different houses like Becker. That's seriously messed up. The kid can't remember where he is when he wakes up every morning."

"I guess mine's not that bad."

"So spill." Ethan plopped onto the couch just like old times.

As Luke sorted through the video games on the coffee table, he told Ethan about Lightning.

"That's not so bad," Ethan said. "Your dad'll come around. Are you and Megan a thing now?"

"No!"

Ethan shrugged. "You hang out with her a lot."

"We work together that's all. Besides she's new to the area."

"Well, the kids at school think you're going out."

"We're not."

Ethan acted like he didn't believe him. "Could be to your advantage. I hear Grace is jealous."

"Grace? She hates me."

"Exactly."

Luke threw a pillow at him.

Ethan ducked. "Hey, look it's Frogger™. Come on, let's squish some frogs."

"You're supposed to *not* get squished." Luke plugged the game in.

"Really? Where's the fun it that?"

Turns out fun could be had with getting a frog safely across a busy street. If he'd played the game alone, Luke doubted he have this much fun. Good thing Ethan didn't hold a grudge, and they were friends again.

Luke clutched his guidance counselor's summons as he walked through the school's hallways. *What did I do wrong?* He couldn't think of anything.

Principal Weaver left the guidance office before Luke reached it. His heart thumped in double time. *Must be in big trouble. Did they think I cheated with my science fair project?* But that had been two weeks ago. They would have said something then. *Right?*

Mrs. Miller must have seen the panic on Luke's face. "Relax, Luke, you're not in trouble. Sit down."

Luke sat on the edge of his seat, hugging his backpack to his chest.

"The reason I called you in here is because you've been absent fifteen days this year," Mrs. Miller said.

"But my father—" Luke started.

"Yes, I know your father calls. And you're never out more than two days at a time, so you don't need a doctor's note. But I'm concerned."

Oh no, that doesn't sound good. He dug his fingers into his pack.

"My grades—" Luke tried again.

"Are fine, I know. Are you having any problems at home?"

"No. No problems." Except for the dog issue. In fact, he and Dad talked a lot more since they'd worked on his science fair project together.

"I see." Mrs. Miller glanced at her computer. "Luke, I've reviewed your history, including the circumstances surrounding your mother's death."

Luke slid back in his chair, bracing for the sympathy he didn't need nor want.

"I noticed that all your absences this year were on days when the weather was bad. So I've done some research and discovered a phobia called Severe Weather Phobia or SWP for short."

Luke opened his mouth to protest, to tell her he didn't have this SWP thing. But deep down he hated being so scared of the weather all the time. "Other people have it?" Hope fluttered in his chest.

"Yes," Mrs. Miller said. "They're afraid to go outside during stormy weather, and they're glued to the Weather Channel. One mother was so terrified that she refused to pick her daughter up from soccer practice during a rainstorm."

"Oh," Luke said. Maybe he wasn't such a scaredy-cat after all.

"Your mother died during a thunderstorm. Do you think that's why you're afraid, Luke?"

"No. I've always been afraid. My mom..." He swallowed. "My mom just proved I'm right to be scared."

"But the odds—"

"I know them all by heart, Mrs. Miller. It doesn't matter, there is always that one person. The one in a million. No one ever thinks about that poor guy."

"True. However, what are the odds that it will happen to two people from the same family?"

Even slimmer, but... "My mom wasn't supposed to be out in the storm. I called her to pick me up early because I was scared. You see? It's my fault she died." He clamped his hand over his big mouth. Why did he just say that? Thinking the words and saying the words were two different things.

Her expression changed to a softer, sadder look. "No one believes it's your fault." She held up her hand, stopping him. "However, you do, so we need to address that as well as your fear of the weather. Unfortunately I'm not trained for either issue. I'd like to call your father to discuss different options."

"Different options?"

"There are other people who are qualified to help you."

"Oh." Luke mulled it over. Dad believed it was Luke's fault, and he had ignored Luke's fears as well. Luke couldn't talk to Dad about it, but maybe if Mrs. Miller called, Dad would let him talk to someone who could help. Dad might say no, but at least he'd tried.

"Okay."

Biking home from Willajean's, Luke was surprised when Dad drove past him, then parked ahead. Ranger poked his head out of the back window. Luke slowed down. Balancing with his hands off the handlebars, he quickly pushed Lightning down into his pack and zipped it shut, leaving only a one-inch opening for the dog to breathe.

He stopped beside the car. His father rolled down the passenger side window.

"What's up?" Luke asked as he silently prayed Lightning would keep quiet.

His father popped the trunk and got out of the car. "Put your bike in the trunk."

"What for?" *Did Dad spot Lightning?* Luke gripped the handlebars hard.

"We need to talk."

Fear flared in Luke's gut as he put his bike in the car. He turned his back to the car for a moment. He opened his backpack, gave Lightning the quiet signal, and zipped it again. Not knowing what to do with it, he placed the backpack behind the passenger seat. Lightning's black nose pressed against the opening. Ranger pawed and whined at the bag.

"What's the matter, boy?" Dad asked the dog.

"I've got some cookies in the pocket of my pack," Luke explained. True, except they were Willajean's special dog treats.

They drove for awhile, and then Dad said, "I got a call from your school today."

CHAPTER 15

Dinosaur Hunting

It had been a week since Luke had talked to the guidance counselor. *She acted fast.* Too worried to look at Dad, Luke peered at the road ahead.

"Some school shrink phoned. Mrs. Muller?"

"Miller," Luke said.

"Yeah, Miller. She said you missed a lot of school. Three weeks." He whistled. "I didn't think it was that much."

Luke glanced at him, trying to gauge his mood.

"Anyway, she spouted some psychobabble about something called *storm phobia*, and how I need to take you to a professional to help you overcome your fears."

Luke waited a moment for his father to go on, but

the silence continued.

"And, what" – Luke cleared his suddenly dry throat – "did you tell her?"

"Just because you're afraid, doesn't mean you have some disorder," Dad said. "I'm afraid of getting electrocuted. I check the power two, three times before I'll start a job. My buddies call me paranoid, but I don't care. And I don't need to see some shrink."

Dad stopped, but he hadn't answered Luke's question. *Should I ask again?*

"What I'm saying is everybody's afraid of something." Dad paused and rubbed his eyebrow with his fingertips. "Your mother hated driving on highways. She'd go twenty miles out of her way just to avoid a highway."

Mom had died on a backcountry road, surrounded by farm fields. Just a couple trees along the road, including the one she'd slammed into. Talk about odds. Luke squeezed his eyes shut, trying to hold back the tears that threatened.

"Was Mom afraid of anything else?" Luke asked.

There was a long pause before Dad said, "Yes. She was afraid of losing you and your brothers. She would dress you boys in super bright neon T-shirts when she took you to Hersheypark so she could spot you. She wouldn't let you go on the bigger rides even though you were bored with the kiddie rides." Dad laughed. "I had to sneak you on with me and your brothers, and tell her about it later."

"I remember Mom yelling at you for taking me on the SooperDooperLooper."

"Yeah, she was overprotective." Dad pulled the car into their driveway and turned off the engine. He made no move to get out. "She loved you kids so much. In fact, the night…she died, she already had her keys in her hands and was heading out the door when you called."

Luke's heart froze in mid-beat.

Dad met Luke's gaze. "Do you understand what I'm saying? She already planned to go and get you. It's not your fault. I don't blame you."

A thousand emotions slammed into Luke. His head spun. He stared at Dad as if seeing him for the first time. "Why didn't you tell me this before?"

"I couldn't. It's…taken me this long to sort it all out. It's still very hard for me to talk about her." He sucked in a deep breath. "And I thought you were just mad at me about the puppy and didn't really believe I blamed you. Not until Mrs. Miller called."

"Oh." All this was too much to take in.

"I don't blame you. It's not your fault. Okay, buddy?"

"Ah…okay." He guessed. Dad had dumped a ton on him. Luke needed to sit down alone and unravel the tangle inside him.

"Now that we have that settled, there's still the other problem."

Confused, he asked, "The puppy?"

"No, your fear of the weather."

"Oh."

"I told Mrs. Miller that your fear is just a stage. That I didn't have the money for some fancy doctor to tell me that you'll grow out of it."

"But it's been years, Dad."

"Do you remember when you were convinced a Tyrannosaurus rex hid under your bed?"

Luke couldn't forget the nightmares of being chased through the woods by the monster. Feeling the ground shake as the beast's thundering feet drew closer, looking back to see T. rex's twelve-inch-long, serrated teeth gleaming in the moonlight.

"Remember how I went dinosaur hunting every night to convince you he wasn't there, and we rigged up an under-the-bed light to keep him away?"

Luke smiled. Dad had worn a goofy hat and slung a water rifle over his shoulder. He called himself Great Bwana as he crept around the room and dived under the bed skirt with the rifle in his hands.

"Eventually you grew out of it and didn't need me to check your room. This is a stage, too. It's just taking longer." Dad clapped him on the shoulder. "But no more days off, buddy. I'll drive you to school if the weather's bad. Okay?"

Luke nodded, not sure what to say. Just the thought of Dad driving in the rain scared him. But Dad made a good point. His fear could be a stage. Although Mrs. Miller had also made sense. The tangle inside him grew tighter.

And the knowledge that Luke still checked under his bed for the T. rex lay heavily on him.

Rain pelted the windows, and the panes shook with each blast of wind. Luke read his history book, but the words didn't make sense. Thunder rumbled. He clutched the edge of his desk with sweaty hands. Each flash of lightning sent a pulse of fear through his body.

Finally Luke asked Mr. DeWire if he could be excused. He snatched the hall pass and bolted into the hallway.

Now what? The safest place is an interior room

without windows.

Luke found a storage closet, slipped inside, and closed the door. As the storm passed over the school, he sweated it out. He wished Dad had agreed to send him to talk to a counselor or shrink. Would Mrs. Miller be able to help without Dad's permission? He couldn't keep this up. His stomach hurt all the time, and he dreaded watching the Weather Channel. Spring in Pennsylvania meant every day had a chance for a thunderstorm.

When the bell rang, Luke had to get to his next class or be marked late. He eased open the door and joined the flow of students. Hopefully no one spotted him. Mr. DeWire said nothing about his long absence from class when Luke returned the hall pass. Luke wondered if Mrs. Miller had talked to his teachers about his SWP.

At the end of the day, Megan cornered him. "I saw you sneaking out of that closet."

He sighed. "Did anyone else see me?"

"I don't know. But, Luke, you need to talk to someone." She gestured at him. "You're a mess. Convince your dad."

Megan was right. Deep down Luke agreed. Every night he planned to ask Dad, and every night he chickened out.

After hiding in the storage closet for the third time that March, Luke decided to talk to Mrs. Miller again. Maybe she could convince Dad.

"I've tried," Mrs. Miller said when he visited her after school. "Your father is convinced your fears are temporary."

Luke slouched in the chair. His heart-thumping

panic didn't feel temporary.

What am I going do? Save money and hire my own shrink?

"Is there any other way?" he asked. "Another guidance counselor?"

She leaned back and tapped a pencil on his file. "There's a counselor at the high school. I've discussed your phobia with him. Not by name," she added quickly. "He has experience with this type of problem. Would you like to talk to him?"

Would he?

What if the guy couldn't help? What if he made it worse? What if someone at school found out and teased him?

Luke swallowed all those questions back down into his churning stomach.

"Sure."

Hershey High School was just down the road from the middle school. Standing outside the main doors, Luke studied the map Mrs. Miller had given him. Mr. Hedge's office looked easy to find. Luke eyed the few high schoolers leaving for the day. The guys looked…big and brawny and mean.

A couple had mustaches, and one had a full beard. Maybe he should just go. If Jacob and Scott caught him here…

No. He pushed all those thoughts away. Determined, Luke followed the directions and knocked on Mr. Hedge's door.

"Come in," a man called.

Luke entered a small neat office.

Mr. Hedge stood and shook his hand. "Have a seat, Luke."

Perching on the edge of the chair with his backpack on his lap, Luke studied Mr. Hedge as the counselor settled behind the desk. Mr. Hedge wore a pink polo shirt, khaki pants, and thick round eyeglasses. Only a thin strip of graying hair stretched from ear to ear. Mr. Hedge didn't match Luke's vision of a shrink at all. He'd expected an old guy with a bow tie and suspenders.

"I've read through your files and Mrs. Miller's comments." Mr. Hedge flipped a few pages over. "Now I could spout some psychobabble and promise you I can cure you, but the truth is I can't do anything."

Luke's heart sank.

"But you can," Mr. Hedge said.

Confused, Luke peered at the counselor.

"To get over your fears, *you're* going to have to do all the work. You're going to dig deep inside you and expose things that you don't want to. Voice those inner thoughts no matter how nasty and evil. I will promise you that what you say in this room goes no further. You won't get into trouble." He lowered his voice. "You can even curse in here. I do. See that?" He pointed to two red scabs on the tip of his finger. "A staple went right through. Oh man, lots of cursing ensued, believe me."

Luke smiled.

"Do you think you can do that?"

"Curse or staple my finger?" Luke asked.

Mr. Hedge laughed. "Ah, a joker. I like. So do you think you can talk to me?"

Could he? If he didn't want to spend another storm shaking and panting like a frightened dog, he had to do something. "Yes."

"Great! There's something I want to talk about right now."

Uh-oh. Luke hugged his backpack to his chest, bracing for the questions.

"I want to know all about your science fair project. You built weather instruments that worked. How cool is that?"

Talking to Mr. Hedge wasn't as bad as Luke had thought. He didn't know how discussing his science project would help him, but doing *something* felt better than doing nothing.

Luke met with Mr. Hedge twice a week, then headed over to Willajean's to help with the training.

"No, Lightning. Come on. Pay attention," Luke yelled in frustration as the white dog wandered off the course yet again.

Megan and Willajean worked Lance nearby. Megan was training him in air scenting. Lightning followed a person's scent left on the ground, but Lance sniffed the air.

"Dogs see the world through their noses," Megan had explained. "They have one million scent receptors per nostril. And did you know, people shed about forty thousand dead skin cells a *minute*? That's so gross, but that's what Lance is smelling – those skin cells when they're blown downwind from the person."

Luke rubbed his fingers along his arm. Losing forty thousand cells a minute sounded like he shouldn't have any skin left at all. Really gross.

"Nooooo." Luke groaned as Lightning lay down in the middle of the course again, ignoring him.

"Don't worry, she'll straighten out," Willajean said. "She's ten months old and in her doggy adolescence. Typical teenager, thinks she knows everything." Willajean shot Megan a look. "Give her another year."

"Another year," Luke cried. He'd hoped to enter Lightning into an AKC junior tracking test in the fall. Waiting until next April would take forever.

Willajean laughed. "That's not bad. I'm still waiting for Alayna to straighten out."

"All Alayna wants to straighten is her hair," Megan said.

Luke covered a laugh. Alayna claimed to have too much homework to help in the afternoons. He didn't miss her at all, and he hoped she'd find another job this summer. Maybe Jacob and Scott could get her a job at Hersheypark. That'd be sweet.

Luke biked over to the high school. He'd been confiding in Mr. Hedge about his guilt over Mom's death. Strange they hadn't been talking too much about his fear, but he guessed they'd get to that eventually. And being allowed to say anything no matter how stupid – like Scott grossing him out by chewing with his mouth open – or illogical – like what'd he do if he could control the weather, eased the tight knots inside him. Odd.

Luke didn't bother to knock before entering Mr. Hedge's office. Big mistake. Two other students sat in front of the counselor's desk.

"Sorry," Luke said, automatically backing out. But he stopped as Jacob and Scott turned to look at him.

CHAPTER 16

Guys Don't Chat

What are Jacob and Scott doing here? Did Mr. Hedge rat me out?

His brothers looked serious, but not pissed off. At least, not yet. Uncertain what to do, Luke stayed on the threshold, clutching the doorknob.

"This isn't an ambush, Luke," Mr. Hedge said. "Come on in."

Luke stepped inside. The air pressed on him. Another chair had been placed next to the desk. Luke sat, but kept an eye on his brothers.

"Jacob and Scott have been talking to me for the last three months."

Luke's attention snapped to Mr. Hedge. Not what he'd expected. *About Mom*? "But I thought…" That they were okay.

"Losing a parent is a life-changing event for everyone. No one is immune. Although everyone deals with it differently." Mr. Hedge gave Scott a tight smile.

"Hey, anyone could have set fire to the chem lab," Scott said. "What I want to know is, who's the idiot who thought giving a bunch of teenagers flammable chemicals and Bunsen burners is a good idea? It was just a matter of time."

"Uh-huh. Make sure you tell that to your future parole officer," Mr. Hedge teased.

"And don't forget to include that you're a graduate of Mr. Hedge's twelve-step program," Jacob said.

"Twelve steps?" Mr. Hedge's bushy eyebrows spiked over his glasses.

"Yeah, it's twelve steps from here to the bathroom. It's where we go to flush all that touchy-feely crap you feed us down the toilet." Jacob mimed putting his finger in his mouth.

"Touché." The counselor appeared impressed.

"Uh… What's this have to do with me?" Luke asked.

"Sorry, Luke. Your brothers have a tendency to use humor and sarcasm to avoid difficult subjects. And since *they* wanted to talk to you, I'll go powder my nose." Mr. Hedge headed for the door, but before he left he pointed two fingers at the twins. "No jokes, got it?"

They nodded.

"Good." He closed the door behind him.

Luke grabbed the chair's arms and waited for… *what*? He had no idea. But it couldn't be good. At least Mr. Hedge hadn't ratted him out. Jacob and Scott did that silent twin communication thing.

Finally, Jacob said, "You were right, Luke. We blamed you for Mom's death."

He dug his fingernails into the fabric. How could being right feel so awful?

"You were Mom's favorite. She'd do anything for you, so…yeah, we blamed you," Scott said.

Luke opened his mouth to protest.

Jacob held up his hands. "Don't. We know. We have each other. Dad always worked late. Mom was all you had."

"And Mom was just being Mom." Scott played with the zipper on his jacket.

"Yeah, she would have done the same thing for us. Or Dad. Heck, she'd even risk herself for one of the dogs," Jacob added.

True. Luke remembered Mom tackling Ranger when he was a pup. He'd been about to dash into the busy street, and Mom dived for him, scraping her knees and elbows. They'd been a bloody mess.

"So we've been hashing it out with Hedge," Scott said. He met Luke's gaze. "And we've been real jerks to you. Sorry, Luke. We know it wasn't your fault."

Stunned, Luke studied his brothers. Were they really his brothers, or had aliens taken over their bodies? At this point it was hard to tell.

"We're serious, Luke," Jacob said. "Those thoughts are gone."

"Along with everything you learned today," Scott quipped.

"Excuse me? Who has a ninety-two average? Not you." Jacob poked Scott's arm.

Ah. Not aliens. Too bad. It would have explained a

lot. Luke smiled.

When Mr. Hedge returned, Jacob and Scott immediately stopped picking on each other. Scott put a finger to his lips, signaling Luke to keep quiet about the jokes.

"Did you boys have a nice chat?" the counselor asked.

Jacob rolled his eyes. "Guys don't chat. We took care of business."

"Business?" Scott huffed. "What are you? One of those Mafia guys now?"

Mr. Hedge jumped in before they could start flinging insults again. "You two can go."

Jacob slung his backpack over his shoulder. "You might want to hang out with Hedge, Luke. He's not bad for an old dude."

"Yeah, he doesn't smell like an old man at all. I think it's because the stink of his hemorrhoid cream covers the rot."

"Always a pleasure…" Mr. Hedge shooed the twins out the door. Then he settled behind his desk. "Your brothers wanted to set the record straight so to speak. What do you think?"

"I don't know." Luke relaxed his death grip on the armchair. He thought about what his brothers had said, and the comments Dad had made that day in the car. Did it change anything inside? "My dad, Jacob, and Scott all told me they don't blame me, but *I* blame me."

And once he started talking, Luke couldn't stop the rush of words. "People have been telling me it's not my fault since the accident. And I know I didn't make that particular bolt of lightning strike Mom's minivan. I didn't lose control of the car. I'm not the tree she ran into. But she was out there for me, because she knew I'd be scared."

"What if you had called her and told her to stay home?" Mr. Hedge asked.

"She would have come anyway, and it still would be my fault."

"Okay, so it's your fault. Does it change anything?"

"No."

"You still feel miserable, right?"

"Yes."

"I'll agree that you were the reason she was out there. But you're not the reason she died. It was her choice to be out there – her choice to be a good mom. Did she know it was dangerous to be out during a thunderstorm?"

"Yes, I'd told her a million times!"

"And she knew you were safer inside?"

"Yes, but I was scared. She knew that."

"Scared, but safe. She decided to risk her life by going out in that storm instead of waiting for it to blow over. It was her decision." He leaned forward. "Do you think she'd want you to be so miserable?"

Luke's mind swirled with everything Mr. Hedge had said. But that was the one question he could answer. "No. She'd be baking me cookies, trying to make me feel better. But I can't just turn it off."

"You're right. There's no off button. Too bad, huh? That'd be pretty sweet."

"Yeah."

"But there is a valve, and eventually you can crank that baby down to a trickle. Just like your fear of storms."

"But we haven't even talked about that yet."

"One thing at a time."

Luke groaned. "It's gonna take forever."

"No it won't. Max of four years. Definitely *before* you graduate."

Four years? That *was* forever.

Mr. Hedge studied him a moment. "How about I teach you a few coping techniques, see if they help you during a storm?"

"Okay."

After his session with Mr. Hedge, Luke biked to the kennel and joined Megan in the kitchen. He'd been seeing the counselor for weeks and been talking about his fear of the weather, but despite that and the breathing techniques he learned, Luke still panicked during thunderstorms. And now it was the middle of May – prime time for tornados. At least his brothers had been acting normal. When he actually saw them. Hersheypark opened soon, and then they'd be working as much as possible.

"Sweetie's due any day now," Megan said as she cracked the eggs.

Willajean's favorite papillon would be a happy mother. Then again, when wasn't the dog happy? All Luke had to do was smile at her, and her tail flew.

"Mom and I have bets on which day she'll whelp."

"What did you bet?" Luke asked.

"If I win, Mom has to drive me to school for a week."

"And if you lose?"

"I have to clean out my closet." Megan made an *ugh* face. "Hey do you want to study for the geometry test later?"

"Can't. I'm going to the movies with Ethan." He and Ethan had been hanging out a lot. Just like old times.

"Oh." Megan focused on the bowl.

"Besides, the test isn't until next week." Luke threw a piece of meat to Lightning. She snatched it out of midair.

"Yeah, well, those proofs are hard."

"Call Jenna, she'll help you."

"I guess."

A damp blast blew into the kitchen as Megan's dad entered. He wore a flannel shirt with black jeans and shiny black cowboy boots that looked like they were more suited for a night out than for tromping around a farm.

"Hey, Luke," he said.

"Hey, Mr. Duncan," Luke replied, not comfortable with calling him Max like he'd asked.

Megan's face took on a guarded expression. She chopped the dogs' meat. The knife banged loudly with each stroke.

"What are you doing here?" Megan asked her dad. "I thought you didn't like the smell of dog." She swept past him with a bowl full of chopped raw liver that glistened in the fluorescent light.

He backed up a step to avoid the bowl. Luke hid his smile.

"Just thought I'd come visit. See why you spend so much time here, Meggie," he said.

"Scoping out the merchandise is more like it," Megan accused. She shoved the bowl into the refrigerator.

Wow. Luke couldn't believe she'd just said that.

"Megan Louise Duncan, don't you ever talk to me that way." Her dad took a step toward her, and she froze.

"The rice is done," Luke said, reminding them he was in the room.

Mr. Duncan relaxed slightly. "Come on, Meggie,

honey. I told you I was sorry. I had too much to drink that night. When I sobered up, I felt awful. But it was too late to apologize. Your mother had already called the cops. What can I do to convince you?"

He must be talking about the night he had stolen Willajean's puppies. He sounded sorry. If Luke hadn't been listening to Megan gripe about her father since Christmas, he might have believed Mr. Duncan.

Megan put her hands on her hips. "You can go back to North Carolina."

Luke held his breath.

Mr. Duncan mimicked Megan's gesture. "I'm not going back. I'll just have to find another way. You'd better get used to me being around. I plan to stay. Fact of life." With that, Megan's dad left the kennel.

Had Mr. Duncan been mocking her, or had she gotten that saying from him? Luke was smart enough not to ask.

Megan stomped around the kitchen, banging doors, and tossing dirty cutting boards into the sink. "I'll show him," she mumbled under her breath.

"How?" Luke asked.

Megan whispered, "The vet is coming tomorrow to microchip all the dogs."

"What does that do?"

"If your dog gets lost and someone finds him, they can scan the chip and trace him back to you. If your dog is stolen, you can prove he's yours. And if he's sold to a research lab with a microchip, they won't take him."

Luke was surprised she'd said something nice about the labs. According to Megan, research labs that used animals for experiments were the ultimate evil.

"How do you know about this?" Luke asked.

"When the vet gave the dogs their shots, I helped her. Dr. Amy told me I should become a veterinarian because I knew so much about dogs." Megan blushed. "Anyway, she told me about the microchips."

"Is it expensive?"

Megan shrugged. "I don't know."

"Does your mom know?"

She shot him a dark look. "The food's done. I need to go in and get ready for supper."

In other words, no, her mom didn't know. The next morning before school, Megan charged into the kennel with the force of a tornado. Slamming doors, she shoved the dogs out of her way and threw bowls down in front of them.

After dodging out of her way for the sixth time, Luke asked, "What's wrong?"

"My mother cancelled the vet visit." Megan spat the words out.

"Why?"

"Too expensive. It costs fifty bucks a dog."

Luke calculated. "That's seventeen hundred dollars."

"Plus the cost for the vet's visit." Megan's shoulders sagged. "But I think the real reason is she doesn't want to hurt Dad's feelings, but I don't care." Megan's eyes turned shiny, and her nose flushed red. "He's why we *need* the microchips."

"He doesn't seem that bad." Luke tried to make her feel better. "He said he was sorry. He went through rehab."

It didn't work. Megan stormed out.

Next time, I'll keep my mouth shut.

At the end of the school day, Megan skipped out the doors. "I checked the web during flex time, and I can microchip the dogs myself," she said in a rush. "I can order a microchip kit and buy extra chips. It only costs five hundred dollars."

He whistled. "Only? Will your mom agree to that?"

"Doesn't matter. I'm going to use my birthday and Christmas money I've been saving for years. Then Mom can't say no."

"Sounds like a plan."

The rest of the week, Megan smiled more and laughed. Just like she used to do before her dad arrived. She came over Luke's house a couple nights to do homework and joked with Dad.

But on Friday morning, Megan wasn't at the kennel. In fact, no one was there. The dogs hadn't been fed, either. Lance was in his crate. Megan's bike was still in the shed, so Luke figured she was sick. Willajean usually came down and told him, but her Jeep was gone. Maybe she'd taken Megan to the doctor.

Luke debated if he should check at the house or ask Alayna at school. But he'd waited too long, and the school bus had already pulled away. If he didn't hurry, he'd be late for school. Luke left without Megan. But he didn't feel right, and he worried about her all day.

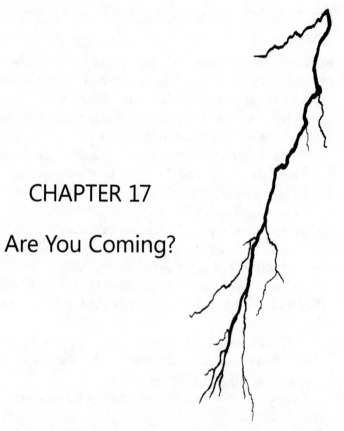

CHAPTER 17

Are You Coming?

After school Luke raced back to the kennel on his bike. Coasting down the long driveway, he spied Dad's car parked at Willajean's house. His heart drummed along with the bike's tires. Dad and Willajean talked on the front lawn.

Lightning.

Dad had found out Luke'd been sneaking the dog home at night. A strange clammy nausea rolled up his throat. To make matters worse, Jacob and Scott leaned against the car. And their three bloodhounds poked their heads out of the car windows.

Huh? Why bring the dogs? Luke didn't have time

to figure it out, because as soon as he stopped his bike, everyone looked at him. His legs turned to mush. An overwhelming desire to bolt flushed through him.

What was going on? Luke clutched his bike for support and walked it toward them.

"Was Megan at school today?" Willajean asked.

Confused, Luke searched her worried expression. Shouldn't she know where Megan was?

"The school called, but we wanted to make sure they hadn't made a mistake," Willajean explained.

"I didn't see her today," Luke said. "Her bike was in the shed this morning. I figured she was sick."

Willajean said nothing, and Dad bit his lip. Finally Luke understood that they weren't mad at him. *Then why… Oh.*

"Where's Megan?" Luke asked.

"I think she ran away last night," Willajean said.

Luke gaped at her. "Are you sure?"

"Now I am. She's not home, and she isn't answering her cell phone."

"Do you know what might have set her off?" Dad asked.

"She had an argument with Max. She ran out of the house around nine o'clock last night," Willajean explained. "I thought she went to the kennel to sleep with Lance. She's been doing that since Christmas. I would have gone after her, but right after the argument, Sweetie started whelping and having complications. I rushed her to the vet."

Luke sucked in a breath.

"Sweetie's fine," Willajean added for Luke's benefit.

"By the time I came home, I assumed Megan had left for school. But the school left a message on my machine.

I spent the entire afternoon looking everywhere I could think of. That's when I phoned you. Megan's always hiking or biking in the woods. It's the only place left that I haven't searched. She could be lost or hurt." For a moment, fear gripped Willajean's face like a clenched fist.

Dad questioned Willajean about what Megan had been wearing last night. "Do you have any family in the area?"

"No."

"Did you call her friends?"

At the last question, Willajean looked at Luke. "Luke's her only friend."

No. That wasn't possible. "What about Jenna?"

"Jenna came out once. Megan's just not into girl things. She's always been more of a tomboy, and besides her friend Karen, she mostly hung out with the boys in our old neighborhood."

Now Luke wished he'd invited Megan along when he hung out with Ethan. Before he'd worked up the nerve to talk to Ethan, he and Megan had spent almost every day together. Guilt mixed with fear. *What if she'd gotten lost in the woods? Or worse yet, what if she'd died?*

"You don't think she intends to stay away?" Dad asked.

"No. If she planned to stay away, she would have taken Lance."

"Where's Max?" Dad asked.

"Gone." Willajean frowned. "He got an animal dealer license. Now he can legally buy and sell animals, even to the research labs. That's what they argued about. After Megan ran off, I asked him to leave."

A gust of wind blew from the east. With Megan

missing, Luke hadn't noticed the line of thunderclouds advancing from the west. The storm fed on the heavy moisture in the air, sucking the wind toward it like a giant vacuum cleaner. Bad timing. The familiar fear swirled in his guts like a mini tornado.

"Dad, a storm is coming," Luke said with a steady voice despite the panic simmering in his heart.

"Then we better hurry and search the surrounding woods before the storm washes away her scent," Dad said.

And with that statement, something shifted in Dad. He went from a regular dad to something…more. He moved with confidence. He kept calm. He seemed capable. Luke marveled. He'd never seen his Dad act this way before. And Luke's fear for Megan eased just a bit.

Unaware of Luke's scrutiny, Dad opened the trunk of his car and unloaded his rescue pack, compasses, and a topographic map of the area. Dad had every topo map of Pennsylvania in an oversized envelope.

"Okay, Willajean, we'll need something with Megan's scent on it. A shirt. Or a shoe would be better."

"Right." Willajean bolted for the house.

"Jacob, take the topo map and break the surrounding area into sections. Use ridges and streams as borders for the sections if you can. Number the sections and highlight any hiking trails, drainage routes, or power lines you find. We'll check the easy walking terrain first before going into the denser woods." Dad handed markers to Jacob.

"Scott, for the first shift, you'll man the command center."

"Command center?" Scott asked, glancing around the farm.

A smile briefly touched Dad's lips. "The car. You'll have the topo map. Because we have only one map, and Jacob and I are going to search different sections, we'll take the compasses and call you for guidance. You'll mark down the coordinates of any clues we find. Okay?"

"Got it," Scott said, but he glanced nervously at Hounddog.

"Is everyone's phone charged?" Dad asked the twins. They all checked their batteries.

"We should have service out here, but if it's spotty, we'll switch to the two-way radios."

While Jacob marked the map, Dad transferred a few supplies to another backpack for Jacob to carry. Then he let the dogs out of the car, and Scott helped him put harnesses on all three. When Willajean returned with Megan's sneaker, Dad let the dogs sniff it.

"Ranger and I will take section one," Dad said. "Jacob, you and Moondoggie check the easy walking routes of section two. Systematic and slow, gets the job done."

The twins had been strangely quiet and serious the whole time, making Luke nervous. Luke's heart squeezed when Dad shouldered his rescue pack. An extensive first aid kit was stashed inside.

This is hardcore.

"What about me?" Luke asked. "I want to help, too."

"You can wait in the kennel in case she comes back for Lance."

"Can you feed and let the dogs out for me?" Willajean asked. "I should be here if Megan returns, and I also need to keep an eye on Sweetie and her pups."

"Okay. Did anyone call the police?" Luke asked.

"They'd just call me," Dad said in a dismissive tone.

"By the time they'd get organized, we'll have found her."

With Ranger in the lead, Dad, Jacob, and Moondoggie headed east while Hounddog stayed with Scott in the car.

Luke ran to the kennel. Lightning danced around his feet as he fed the dogs. Luke hoped Dad would find Megan quickly. His house was east of Megan's farm. Maybe she'd cut through the forest to visit him and had gotten lost. Which meant Dad was on the right track, and Luke shouldn't worry. Except he did.

Letting all the dogs out into their runs temporarily distracted Luke from obsessing about Megan and panicking over the approaching storm. Lance moped and didn't eat much. Megan's dog leaned against Luke's leg to get attention instead of knocking Luke over with affection. Poor pup missed Megan.

Luke guided all the dogs back into their crates and cleaned the runs. A dark gray blanket of clouds sealed the sky. Luke rushed to pick up the piles as the wind rattled the metal fences of the runs. He drew in deep breaths like Mr. Hedge had taught him, trying to calm his racing pulse. Lance and Lightning kept him company. They sniffed around, getting underfoot. After Luke tripped over them for the fourth time, he shooed them out.

In the distance, lightning flashed. Luke clutched the scraper hard and counted the seconds until the crack of thunder.

He had calculated it out once. Thunder was just the sound of the lightning ripping through the air. But light moved so much faster than sound, so a five second delay between the flash of lightning and the thunder equaled one mile. This storm was about seven miles away. No immediate danger. He steadied his breathing. Seven miles meant he still had a couple minutes to get to safety.

Unfortunately Lance and Lightning had disappeared. Calling into the wind, Luke frantically searched for them. Lance arrived when called a second time. Luke put him into his crate. Racing outside, Luke found Lightning digging at a bush near the edge of the woods behind the kennel.

"Come on," Luke said, pulling her away by her collar.

Lightning held a brown flip-flop in her mouth. He took it from her. It was one of Megan's. The toe strap had snapped. Luke looked underneath the bush and grabbed the other one.

Dropping the flip-flops, he dashed back into the kennel's kitchen to check if her work boots were by the door. Megan only wore them in the kennel. No boots, but dried pellets of mud made a pattern on the floor.

She's wearing them. Okay, how does that help find her?

Outside, Lightning barked. With a nervous glance at the darkening sky, Luke hurried to fetch her. She circled Megan's flip-flops with her nose brushing the ground. Then she headed up the trail that snaked pass the lake in the opposite direction from Dad and Ranger. Lightning stopped and looked back at Luke as if to say, "Are you coming?"

Thunder clapped. Luke jumped. The trees creaked and bent in the gusting wind. Any moment now the storm would unleash its full fury. Panicked, Luke remembered the meteorologist on the Weather Channel talking about the five horsemen of thunderstorms. Wind, flood, hail, lightning, and tornadoes all spawned by super storm cells. Dangers ready to trample Luke beneath their feet.

Luke hunched over, resisting the desire to bolt

inside. Fear throbbed through him with each pounding beat of his heart. All the muscles in his body urge him to find shelter. But Megan might be down this path. She could be hurt or in danger. Luke cursed his dad for not getting him a cell phone. He glanced over at the house. Scott could contact Dad.

Luke opened his mouth to call Lightning back, but stopped. No doubt Lighting had Megan's scent. Unafraid, the small white dog wagged her tail under the bending trees. Luke closed his mouth. Megan needed him. Right now. When the rain came, it would wash the scent from the ground. No time to spare.

Luke stepped toward his dog.

Must. His legs wobbled like an uneven tower of blocks.

Find. His stomach pinched tight around a cold hard ball of fear.

Megan. With every nerve tingling, Luke followed Lightning.

CHAPTER 18

Don't Think, Just Do

A step. One foot in front of the other. Luke concentrated on the placement of his feet as if he balanced on a tightrope above a deep chasm. He focused on the white fur ball in front of him. The wind shook the trees so hard they shushed without stop.

Luke ducked his head with each roar of thunder. The limbs above him could break at any moment and crush him like road-kill.

Sweat soaked his jacket, and he sucked in the thick humid air. When Lightning reached the branch in the trail, she veered left, up the hill. Leave it to Megan to pick the steepest trail.

Luke felt electrified, like if he touched something he would cause a spark. He checked the hair on his arms and his head. If the hair stood straight up, it meant the air was charged for a lightning strike. Nothing. For now.

Fat raindrops pelted the forest, splatting as they hit the bushes nearby. A minute later, pouring rain broke through the leafy tree canopy followed by a blinding flash of lightning and immediate crack of thunder right above Luke.

He crouched low with his hands on his knees. Huddled on the ground, he shook as he waited for the heart of the storm to pass. When thunder rumbled a few seconds after the lightning and he hadn't turned into an ash pile, Luke finally staggered to his feet, wiping mud from his face.

I can't do this. Megan can't be out here. Lightning is still a pup. No way she found Megan's scent. It's insane.

Another boom of thunder sent Luke to his knees. The rain stung his shoulders, soaked his hair, and ran down his face. A sense of immediate danger overcame Luke.

Need. To. Go. Back. Now.

He screamed for Lightning. His dog waited for him halfway up the trail. Luke drew breath to yell again when an image of Megan flashed in his mind. What if she was in a lot of pain? What if she was bleeding or had broken bones?

No matter how terrified he was, Luke just couldn't leave Megan alone in the storm.

Don't think. Just do.

He crawled after Lightning. Near the top of the trail, Luke stopped, shielding his eyes from the stinging rain. Lightning turned left and disappeared down the narrow path that led to the overlook. Luke counted seconds between the next flash and the thunder. The storm wasn't as close. Not so dangerous.

Luke pushed to his feet and followed the twisty trail. Water-filled boot prints stamped the ground. They'd been made prior to the rain, and the pattern resembled Megan's.

Hope spurred him on, and he picked up his pace. The thick forest blocked the thin path at times. Pushing through the undergrowth, Luke snagged his jacket on a thorny bush. The barbs cut into his skin as he pulled it out. Pain burned, but he ignored it.

When the path straightened out, Luke slowed. The trail ended soon, but he wasn't sure where. Lightning looped back to him. Her white fur was plastered to her body, and mud coated her legs and belly. She ran around his feet then dashed ahead. Maybe she'd lost the scent. Worry flared in his guts.

As the thunderstorm moved further east, the rain lessened. A brisk, cold wind blew from the west. Soaked down to his underwear, Luke shivered. Another line of thunderstorms might be coming. The need to hurry pulsed in his heart.

Lightning returned and sat down next to him. Disappointment wrapped around Luke like a soggy blanket. She had lost the scent. And it was getting dark. Two things *not* in Megan's favor.

Their search for Megan had been for nothing. As Dad would say, a bad rescue. Those words sent a cold knife of fear into Luke.

When Dad found a missing person too late or not at all, it upset him for weeks. Luke had never really thought about it before. But now that Megan was lost, he understood how Dad had felt – sick to his stomach.

It won't happen to Megan. I won't let it.

Determined to return and help Dad with the search whether he wanted Luke or not, he turned around. But Lightning barked, looped around him, and sprinted in the opposite direction.

Now what? He called her. She barked again. It sounded echoey. She had reached the overlook with the steep drop-off. *Oh no.* Luke ran.

Lightning pawed at the edge of the cliff. Luke grabbed her before she could fall.

He hugged her tight. "Don't scare me like that."

A weak flash of light drew him closer to the edge. He peered over.

"Megan," he yelled.

Crouched on the small ledge below, she waved a mud-covered flashlight. Her father lay next to her.

"Luke," she called. "Help! My father broke his leg. It's bad!"

For a second Luke froze as all his thoughts jumbled together. Then the little bit of training Dad had taught him kicked in.

First rule, keep calm. Second, assess the situation. Stuck on a ledge, Megan wore a T-shirt and jeans, and Mr. Duncan had on khakis and a flannel shirt. Both were soaked and shivering in the chilly air – maybe hypothermic. And Mr. Duncan needed medical care.

Third, plan a course of action. Call for help. Did Megan have her cell phone? Dumb question. If she or Mr. Duncan had a working phone, they'd have called last night.

Think. Mr. Duncan couldn't move. But Megan could. *I'll help her first, then we'll go fetch Dad.*

Putting Lightning down, Luke peeled off his wet jacket and wrung it out. He lay down and hooked his feet around a nearby tree trunk. Then he lowered the jacket to Megan.

"Grab it and climb up," he ordered. Rain hit the back of his neck like tiny needles of cold.

On tiptoe, she wrapped her hands around the end of the sleeve. He held on tight while she climbed. Water flowed over the edge and down the side. Her foot slipped, sending rocks and mud onto her father.

Megan tried again. Sliding down, she almost yanked the jacket from Luke's grasp. She grabbed a rock just in time, stopping her fall. No longer cold, Luke adjusted his hold.

That was close.

"This isn't going to work," she puffed. "I tried before and almost fell off the ledge."

"Keep going," Luke said. "Don't think, just do."

When she was almost within reach, the jacket started ripping.

"Hurry," Luke urged.

Grunting with effort, Megan grabbed Luke's arms.

"Climb up me," he said through gritted teeth.

She did, pulling herself up and over the edge. Luke rolled over, and they both lay on the ground catching their breath.

Luke stood up first. Mud covered him from the neck down. He tried to wipe it off, but only smeared it. Instead, he cleaned off his jacket and handed it to Megan.

She jumped to her feet. "Luke, you came out in a storm."

"Yeah. So?" he said casually, but he couldn't stop grinning. He had faced a storm and hadn't backed down.

"So?" She hugged him. "So, thanks!"

He squeezed her back. "Come on, we need to get help for your dad."

"No. I'll stay here while you get help." She put on his jacket.

"You're coming. You're freezing, and you need to get warm."

She put her hands on her hips. "I'm staying."

Mr. Duncan called from below. They leaned over the edge to hear him. "Meggie, go. Luke's right," he said with effort. "Stop arguing and get moving."

"No."

Luke tried another tactic. "Megan, I am the finder, and you are the findee. You *have* to listen to me. Fact of life."

Not waiting for a response, Luke grabbed her arm and hurried her along the path. Lightning trotted next to them.

Megan picked up Lightning, lavishing hugs and praise on her before setting her down. "I thought she'd run away when I saw her looking down at us," Megan said. "I told her to get help. Dad's cell phone broke when he fell, and I left mine in my pack. Lightning disappeared but came back too fast, so I thought no one would ever find us." Her words rushed out in one burst.

"What were you doing out here?" he asked.

"Last night, I got mad and ran off. I grabbed my backpack and was headed toward your house when my flip-flop broke." Megan gestured at her boots.

"I left my pack on the trail to go change into my boots. While I was in the kennel, guess who came looking for me?"

"Your dad?"

"Yeah. Last person I wanted to see. So I grabbed the flashlight, slipped out the back door, and headed up my trail."

"And ditched your flip-flops in a bush."

"How'd you know that?"

"Lightning found them," he said. "That's how she found you."

"Oh. At least I did one thing right last night." Megan kept quiet for a few steps. "Anyway my dad followed me up the trail, he didn't have a flashlight, but the moon was bright. I tried to trick him by cutting down that path to the overlook." She bit her lip. "I tricked him all right, but not the way I wanted. He was supposed to keep going on the main trail. Instead he came barreling down that path and right over the cliff."

CHAPTER 19

Fact of Life

Luke and Megan hustled down the trail. Lightning lagged behind. The little dog was tired. Luke picked her up and carried her. They bypassed the kennel, heading straight toward the house. As soon as they reached it, Megan let out a small *ah* sound and ran inside.

Luke aimed for Dad's car. The rain had stopped... sometime. Too focused on his task, he hadn't noticed before. Scott was using a flashlight to read the topo map that he'd spread out in the back seat.

"Where've you been?" he asked, without looking up from his map. Before Luke could answer, he said, "Dad found Megan's backpack." He pointed to a spot on the topo. "She's east, but Ranger lost her scent—"

"I found her," Luke said.

Scott finally looked up. "What?"

"Megan's home. Call Dad. Tell them to come back. Mr. Duncan fell and broke his leg. He needs help."

Confusion creased Scott's face. His blond hair looked white in the moonlight.

"Call Dad, I'll explain later."

"How did you find her?" Scott asked.

"My dog tracked her," Luke said proudly.

Scott noticed the white bundle in Luke's arms. Lightning had fallen asleep.

"Call Dad."

"Yeah." Scott picked up his cell phone just as Willajean and Megan joined him.

Megan still wore Luke's wet jacket.

"Go get changed," Luke said to her.

"I've tried to reason with her," Willajean said.

"Not until Dad's okay," Megan replied. "It's my fault he's hurt."

"Don't worry. I'm taking care of it." Luke glared at Megan. "Go inside."

His tone made both Scott and Willajean glance at him in surprise. He sounded just like Dad, and if Luke hadn't been exasperated with Megan, he might have laughed. But the flat tone worked.

"Dad's calling an ambulance," Scott said after Megan and Willajean retreated to the house. "He's on his way."

Luke's arms ached from the weight of Lightning, but he didn't want to wake her. Besides her body heat kept his arms and chest warm. A gust of wind cut right through Luke. He shuddered.

Noticing the motion, Scott said, "You're soaked." Then after a heartbeat, he asked, "Were you out in the storm?"

Luke nodded. His teeth chattered. Scott popped the trunk, took out a blanket, and wrapped it around Luke. He helped Luke sit in the back seat of the car. Lightning stirred once then closed her eyes. Luke covered her with a section of the blanket. Even with the blanket, all his muscles shook. From the cold or just a reaction, he couldn't tell.

When Dad and Jacob returned, Scott slid out to greet them. After a few minutes, Dad opened the car door and frowned at Luke.

"You know you shouldn't have gone out alone, right?" he asked.

"Yes."

"You know it was just dumb luck that you found her? And you know never *ever* to do it again?"

"Yes." Although it wasn't dumb luck. Despite her stubborn streak, Lightning was a smart dog, and a quick learner.

Lightning stood and stretched. Dad glanced at the dog, but didn't comment.

"Where's Megan?" Dad asked.

"In the house."

"Where's Max?"

"I'll show you." Luke stepped from the car, letting Lightning down.

Willajean returned with a pile of sandwiches and three dry jackets for them. Luke wolfed down two before taking a breath to say *thank you*.

Willajean smiled at him. She had been calm during this whole ordeal. Dad had often grumped about worried parents being in the way, but Willajean aided their efforts. Not that she didn't care. The tight lines along her forehead had returned.

When the last sandwich was gone, Dad stationed Jacob at the command center, and called the dogs. Lightning joined in. A mere cotton ball next to the big bloodhounds. The dogs sniffed each other nose to tail.

"Let's go," Dad said, handing a flashlight to Luke.

"Wait a second," Luke said. "You'll need rope and a stretcher. Mr. Duncan won't be able to walk."

"It's all in my pack. Let's hurry. It's not getting any warmer."

Dad took the lead while Luke, Scott, and the dogs trailed behind. The slope seemed steeper this time. The mud on Luke's clothes weighed a ton.

Reaching the top first, Dad paused. "Which way?"

Luke led them along the narrow path and pointed to where Mr. Duncan had fallen.

"How's it going, Max?" Dad called, shining his flashlight over the edge.

The reply was weak. Luke strained, but still couldn't understand it.

"Hold on a little longer. We'll have you out of there in no time."

In a whirlwind of activity, Dad unpacked his gear, tied ropes with pulleys and winches around the trees, and pulled out first aid supplies.

"Point both lights down on us," Dad ordered Luke before he shouldered a climbing harness and shimmied to Mr. Duncan.

Luke directed the two beams onto the men below. A distant flash to the west caught his attention. He counted seconds until the rumble reached him. The thunderstorm was eight miles away.

Concern that the storm would hinder the rescue

was Luke's first reaction. In fact, the familiar panic failed to grip him as hard. Despite his hammering heart, he clutched the flashlights tighter, refusing to give in to the fear.

"Scott, I need the first aid kit and wooden splits," Dad yelled.

While Scott lowered a bucket of supplies, Jacob called to say the ambulance had arrived and the paramedics would meet them on the main trail. From his post by the cliff's edge, Luke watched Dad check Mr. Duncan's vital signs and immobilize his leg.

"Nasty break, Max," Dad said. "But I've seen worse. Don't worry."

Megan's father grunted in pain as Dad attached a climbing harness to him. Then Dad hoisted Mr. Duncan up onto his shoulders in a firefighter's carry position and clipped the injured man to his own harness.

Dad held onto the rope, Scott and Luke cranked the hand winch and pulley system. Luke used every ounce of strength to push the handle toward Scott, who pushed it back. Each crank brought the men up a couple inches. After an eternity the two men reached the top. Following Dad's orders, Scott and Luke unhooked Mr. Duncan and helped him lie on the stretcher, which looked like a canvas sling with handles.

Dad handed Luke a couple white plastic bags.

"Ice packs?" he asked.

"Warmers. Break and shake." Dad covered Mr. Duncan with a thermal blanket.

Luke broke the plastic sacks inside the bags to mix the chemicals together. Warmth emanated from the sacks. Scott tucked them under Mr. Duncan's blanket, while Luke shook some more.

Dad repacked his equipment in record time. Shouldering his pack, Dad paused. "Scott, can you help me carry him? He's about one eighty."

"Sure."

Dad faced front with his back to Mr. Duncan and grabbed the handles, while Scott took the other end.

"On three," Dad said. "One, two, three."

They lifted the stretcher.

"Luke, take the lead with those flashlights."

Luke hurried into position and illuminated the tight trail. The paramedics took over as soon as they reached the main trail. Dad stayed with them until they loaded Mr. Duncan into the ambulance.

Luke stared at his dad in amazement. During this whole ordeal, Dad didn't hesitate, he never acted uncertain about what to do, he didn't complain about the weather or about being exhausted or soaked. Dad had a job to do, and he put his heart and soul into getting Mr. Duncan to safety. Satisfaction lit Dad's face when the ambulance sped away.

Now Luke understood why search and rescue was so important to Dad. Pride filled his chest. His dad had made a difference.

With Megan tucked in close to her and a big grin spread across her face, Willajean stopped them when they reached the car. "Come on inside for some hot chocolate before you leave."

"What about Max?" Dad asked.

"The hospital staff can take care of him."

"All right. We'll finish up here and be right in."

After all the dogs were rewarded with plenty of

praise and the equipment returned to the trunk, Dad put the three bloodhounds into the car, and Luke carried Lightning back to the kennel for a well-deserved rest.

Sad that he wouldn't be able to smuggle her home tonight, he was also relieved, because she needed a bath. So did he. Half-dried mud caked his shoes, jeans, and shirt. Outside, Luke knocked off as much dirt as possible before entering the house.

Inside the warm kitchen they all sat around the table, drinking steaming mugs of hot chocolate and eating blueberry muffins. Luke gawked at the clock. Ten minutes after ten. It felt like only a couple hours had passed not six and a half.

Alayna joined them. Another surprise, because she'd been doing an excellent job of avoiding Luke for months.

Scott jumped up. "Here, have my seat."

She smiled at him, and he gave her a goofy grin. Megan rolled her eyes.

"Luke, why didn't you tell us Megan has a beautiful older sister?" Jacob asked. "We could have shown you around school. We know *all* the shortcuts."

"I'm still learning my way around," Alayna said. "Maybe you can show me tomorrow?"

The twins quickly agreed. Megan made a disgusted face behind their backs.

"To the successful rescue," Willajean said, raising her mug and stopping the teens' flirting. "For which I'm very grateful."

Cup clunked cup as everyone agreed.

"To Megan for keeping her dad comfortable while waiting for rescue," Dad said.

More clunks.

"To Luke for finding me," Megan said.

"Despite the thunderstorm," Scott added.

"A true Storm Watcher," Willajean said.

They laughed as they banged mugs, sloshing hot chocolate onto the table. Luke's cheeks burned. To cover his embarrassment, he said, "To Lightning, who led me right to Megan."

Everyone but Dad raised a cup. Luke's good mood died. *How could Dad still be so stubborn? Lightning proved her worth tonight, and she had no trouble keeping up with the bloodhounds.*

Luke pushed away from the table. Maybe he should check on the dogs before they left. He turned to leave.

Then Dad said, "I guess the little pup can keep coming home with you at night."

Luke spun. "You know?" Amazement mixed with fear. Why wasn't Dad yelling at him?

"Of course. I don't vacuum with my eyes closed. What else would leave clumps of white fur all over your room?"

"To fathers," Megan said quietly. "Even the dumb ones who follow their daughters over cliffs."

They clunked their cold, almost empty mugs.

When Luke glanced at her in surprise, she added, "Talking is the only thing you can do when you're stuck on a cliff with someone for twenty-four hours. Oh, and Mom, Dad got that animal dealer's license because he needed it for his new job."

Now it was Willajean's turn to look shocked. "Really?"

"Yeah, he's gonna be working over at the horse auction in New Holland."

Willajean snorted. "I'll believe it when I see it."

"He won't be able to work for a couple weeks," Dad said. "The doctor at the hospital should be able to tell you how he's doing." He stood up. "We should go so you can check on him."

"He's a big boy," Willajean said. "He can wait and wonder about where I am for a change. I guess he'll be staying in the barn for awhile longer." Willajean paused with a sly grin. "Maybe I'll actually turn the electricity on for him."

Dad laughed. "Now don't be spoiling the boy."

Luke exchanged a glance with his brothers. None of them had heard Dad laugh since Mom died. Dad might not be the perfect father, and Luke dreaded those bad days when Dad's grief affected them all. But there were good days too.

All four of them were working to crank that valve down to slow their pain to a trickle. Maybe they'd become a family again. It'd take time and effort. But everything worth doing did.

Fact of life.

About the Author

Maria V. Snyder switched careers from meteorologist to novelist when she began writing the New York Times best-selling Study Series (Poison Study, Magic Study, and Fire Study) about a young woman who becomes a poison taster. Maria earned a Bachelor of Science degree in Meteorology from Pennsylvania State University. She worked as an environmental meteorologist until boredom and children drove her to write down the stories that had been swirling around in her head. Writing proved to be more enjoyable, and Maria returned to school to earn a Master of Arts in writing from Seton Hill University. Unable to part company with Seton Hill's excellent writing program, Maria is currently a teacher and mentor for the MFA program.

However, Maria's meteorological degree did not go to waste. And to prove it to her parents... er... because she is still fascinated with the weather, she played with the weather while writing Storm Watcher. Weather is also important in her award-winning Glass Series (Storm Glass, Sea Glass, and Spy Glass) about a magician who captures magic inside her glass creations.

Maria lives with her family and a black cat named Valek (a.k.a. the bug assassin!) in Pennsylvania where she is hard at work on her next book. Readers are welcome to check out her website for book excerpts, free short stories, maps, blog, and her schedule at www.MariaVSnyder.com. Maria also loves hearing from her readers and can be contacted at maria@mariavsnyder.com. For fun activities connected with Storm Watcher, readers can go to the special Storm Watcher Kennel site at www.stormwatcherkennel.com.

Lightning ⚡

For More *Storm Watcher* Fun

Go to the Storm Watcher Kennel site:

www.stormwatcherkennel.com

LUKE'S

WEATHER

NOTEBOOK

(IMPORTANT FACTS ABOUT ALL KINDS OF WEATHER)

Five Horsemen of Thunderstorms

The most dangerous clouds are cumulonimbus clouds. These thunderstorm clouds are called "weather factories." They cause wind, hail, lightning, tornadoes, and even flooding. These five weather events are called the five horsemen of thunderstorms.

Below is a look at how each of these horsemen ride across the sky to create storms.

Wind

A thunderstorm is like a giant vacuum cleaner. As the storm grows, it sucks up the warm moist air near the ground. The upward-moving air is called an updraft. Once this column of air reaches 20,000 to 40,000 feet in the sky, it cools and descends. Then it's called a downdraft.

The leading edge, or front, of the downdraft is called the forward-flank downdraft. This is what shakes the leaves on the trees as a thunderstorm approaches. The rear-flank downdraft is the back edge of the storm.

Downdrafts can be intense. They may slam to the ground with gusts that are stronger than hurricanes (75+ miles per hour). These are called downbursts. Tiny ones are called microbursts. Some microburst winds have been clocked above 120 miles per hour (mph). The highest microburst ever recorded was measured at 149.5 mph at Andrews Air Force base in Washington, DC, in 1983.[1]

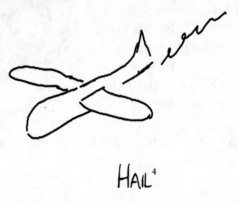

Hail[4]

Hail is a ball of ice that forms inside a thunderstorm. As the warm moist air rises, the air cools and condenses. This creates droplets of water that freeze. These frozen raindrops are called graupel. They get caught in the updrafts and downdrafts. Each time they ride an updraft, they gain another layer of ice. Over time, the hail gets too heavy to stay in the air. So it falls to the ground.

Powerful thunderstorms with strong updrafts can "hold" hail up longer than weaker storms. Strong storms also produce large hailstones. To make a 1" hailstone, the updraft must be at least 50 mph. A 2" hailstone needs close to 70 mph updrafts.

Hailstone Sizes in Inches[2]

0.25 pea
0.50 marble
0.75 penny/large marble/dime
0.88 mothball/nickel
1.00 quarter
1.25 half-dollar
1.50 walnut
1.75 golf ball
2.00 hen egg
2.50 tennis ball
2.75 baseball
3.00 tea cup
4.00 grapefruit
4.50 softball

The largest hailstone recorded landed in Vivian, South Dakota, on July 23, 2010. This hailstone was about the size of a volleyball. It weighed 1.94 pounds and was 18.6" around.[3]

Strange things have been found inside hail. Twigs, leaves, pebbles, nuts, and even insects have been trapped inside.

LIGHTNING (AND THUNDER)

Lightning is called *thunderstorm electrification* in weather language.

Lightning lives in the center of a thunderstorm where the air moves fast. Frozen raindrops ride the air currents like a roller coaster. Some of the drops are going up, rising on updrafts. Others are falling, riding downdrafts. With so much movement, the drops sometimes collide. When they do, the raindrop that was going up becomes positively charged. The one going down takes on a negative charge.

 A thunderstorm is like a battery: The top end is positive, and the bottom end is negative.

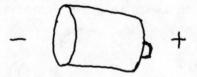

When a thunderstorm is directly overhead, the large negative charge at the base of the storm repels the negative charge on the ground. That causes the ground and any people (or objects) on the ground to become positively charged. These strong opposite charges close together create the electrical discharge (spark) that is lightning. It's like what happens when you shuffle across a rug in your socks. If you then touch a pet or a friend or a metal doorknob, you may get "shocked" by a spark. That spark and shock are tiny compared to the ones lightning produces.[23]

The most common forms of lightning are:

- **Cloud-to-cloud:** the strike occurs between clouds
- **Cloud-to-ground:** lightning hits the ground
- **In-cloud:** lightning happens inside the cloud; it often looks like a sheet
- **Cloud-to-air:** a positively charged cloud hits negatively charged air

The brightness of lightning is equal to about 100 million light bulbs going on and off. The temperature of lightning is about 50,000° F. That is around five times hotter than the surface of the sun.[24]

When lightning flickers, it's not just one bolt hitting the ground. It's a series of multiple strikes. The bolts all hit the same spot. Then like a yo-yo, they return to the cloud. Each stroke, or flash, moves at a speed of about 200,000 mph. That's the fastest yo-yo ever. And although it may look thick, a bolt of lightning is only about as wide as a pencil.[11]

Thunder comes from lightning cutting through the air. Remember, the bolt is like a yo-yo. When it travels down, it heats up and expands the air. Then it zings right back to the cloud. It cools and contracts the air as it goes. So thunder comes from air coming and going at terrific speed. Hot and cold, up and down. Everything collides and BOOM! The sky sounds like bowling balls smacking into pins, or like a growling animal.

Light moves faster than sound, so the flash happens

right away. But thunder takes five seconds to travel one mile. Counting to five lets you know how far away the storm is. If you count to five three times, the lightning is three miles away.

TORNADOES

Tornadoes form only in severe (supercell) thunderstorms. The National Weather Services says a severe thunderstorm has hail at least 1" in diameter, and/or wind gusts of 58 mph, and/or a tornado.[5]

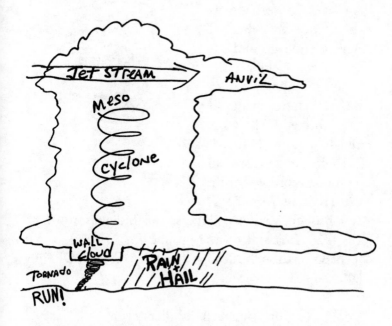

Not all supercells cause tornadoes. The storm must have strong winds in order to produce a tornado. These winds need to blow at different speeds and in different directions at various heights from the ground. This may happen when warm, moist air meets cool, dry air. If the rotating winds are caught in an updraft, they spin faster and tighter. This cone of air becomes a funnel cloud. Once it hits the ground, it becomes a tornado.

The tornado is the most destructive of all storms. But it usually only causes damage in a small area. Winds of over 300 mph have been recorded. Tornadoes can last a few minutes or as long as an hour. Most tornados last about ten minutes.[6]

An average tornado is about 375 feet wide.[7] It stays on the ground for less than 1 mile. The widest tornado on record was 2.6 miles wide. It tore through El Reno, Oklahoma on May 31, 2013. The longest tornado path on record was from the Tri-State Tornado. It  cut through Missouri, Illinois, and Indiana on March 18, 1925. It stayed on the ground for 219 miles. This tornado was also the deadliest tornado on record, killing 695 people.[6]

Cool picture of a supercell thunderstorm:
http://icons-ak.wxug.com/i/severe/supercell_explainer.png

Great website for more info about tornadoes:
http://www.spc.noaa.gov/faq/tornado/index.html

Tornado Safety:
http://www.spc.noaa.gov/faq/tornado/safety.html

FLASH FLOODS

Think about when you overfill a glass with water. Water flows over the rim, and maybe on to the floor and your shoes. That's like a mini-flash flood. The same thing happens in streams and rivers. When it rains too hard, water spills out over the banks. If enough water flows out and has nowhere to go, it causes a flash flood. These floods are dangerous.

Moving water packs a punch. People are often surprised by the power of moving water. It takes only 2' of water to sweep a car away. Only 6" of fast-moving floodwater can knock you over.[11]

On June 9, 1972, the Black Hills flash flood in South Dakota dumped 15" inches of rain in 5 hours. Rapid Creek overflowed and killed 238 people.[25]

The worst flash flood on record was the Johnstown, Pennsylvania Flood. On May 31, 1889, heavy rains caused the South Fork Dam to burst. A wall of water swept through the town, killing 2,209 people.[8]

When Thunder Roars, Go Indoors!

Lighting kills. According to the National Weather Service, next to flooding, it is the second deadliest weather-related killer. About 73 deaths occur each year from lightning strikes. That's more than from snowstorms, tornadoes or hurricanes.[9]

If you can hear thunder, then you're within striking distance of a thunderstorm's deadly lightning. The safest and smartest thing to do is go inside. Find a substantial building or a hard-topped vehicle right away. Always bring your pets inside with you. Picnic shelters, bus stops, dugouts, tents, and sheds are NOT safe. Neither are doghouses, treehouses, or other small buildings even without electricity. In a car, don't lean against the doors during a storm.

Avoid touching corded phones. Cell phones are okay. Never touch windows, doors, plumbing, or any plugged-in appliances. Don't wash your hands, do the dishes, or take a shower during a thunderstorm. Also don't lie on a concrete floor or lean on a concrete wall. Lightning can travel through the metal rebar inside the concrete.

After a thunderstorm passes, wait thirty minutes before going back outside. The National Weather Service says that if everyone followed these rules, lightning deaths would be reduced.

If you can't find a safe building or vehicle, here are tips to lower your risk of being struck by lightning[10]:

- Avoid open areas and fields
- Do not stand on top of ridges or hills
- Keep away from tall trees, tall objects, or isolated trees
- In a forest, keep close to a lower stand of trees
- Stay away from bodies of water like ponds, lakes, rivers and even wet items
- Stay away from metal objects like fences, poles, and towers

If the hair on your arms, neck, and head stand on end, a lightning strike is coming. Make yourself as small a target as possible. If possible, find a ditch or shallow depression. Crouch down with your feet together. Do NOT put your hands on the ground. Instead, place your hands on your knees. Also do NOT hold hands or hug another person.[11]

12 Curious Facts about Lightning

- Florida is the lightning capital of the United States.
- The most lightning deaths happen during fishing, camping, boating, soccer, and golfing.
- 82 percent of lightning victims are male.
- 70 percent of lightning strikes are during the months of June, July, and August.
- In the United States, about 22 million lightning flashes strike the ground each year.
- Lightning can also strike in the winter during a rare thunder snowstorm.
- People can survive a lightning strike, but many are badly hurt.
- American park ranger Roy Sullivan was struck by lightning seven times between 1942 and 1977. He survived them all. People nicknamed him the *Human Lightning Rod*. He earned a place in the Guinness Book of World Records.
- Lightning strikes can melt sand. The sand turns into glass-like tubes. These are called *fulgerites*.
- Many cloud-to-ground lightning strikes are forked. This means they strike many different points on the ground.
- Once lightning hits the ground, it can spread more than 60 feet from the strike point.
- Fear of lightning is called *keraunophobia*.
- Fear of thunder is called *brontophobia*.

(See endnotes. From sources 9-11, 15)

TEST YOUR KNOWLEDGE OF THUNDERSTORMS

TRUE OR FALSE?

1. Lightning never strikes the same location twice.
2. The rubber tires on a car protect you from lightning.
3. Lightning can start forest fires.
4. A 5-second delay between a flash of lightning and the rumble of thunder means the thunderstorm is 1 mile away.
5. If there aren't any clouds overhead and it's not raining, you're safe from lighting.
6. It's dangerous to use your cell phone during a storm.
7. You're pretty safe inside an airplane during a thunderstorm.
8. If it starts to thunder, you should shelter under a tree.
9. If someone is struck by lightning, do not touch them.
10. If trapped outside during a storm, do not lie on the ground.

ANSWERS

1. False – Lightning will strike the same spot many times. The Empire State Building is struck almost 100 times a year.
2. False – The metal sides and roof of the car protect you, not the tires. The metal conducts the lightning to the ground. During a storm, do NOT lean on the car doors.
3. True – In the Western United States and Alaska, lightning is the main cause of forest fires. In the past, 15,000 lightning strikes have burned more than two million acres of forests across the United States.
4. True – Sound waves travel slower than light waves. You see the flash of light right away. But it takes the sound of thunder 5 seconds to travel 1 mile.
5. False – Lightning can strike more than 3 miles from a thunderstorm. And "bolts from the blue" have hit 10 to 15 miles away from the storm's center.
6. False – You can use a cell phone during a thunderstorm. But you should NOT use a corded phone. Electricity from lightning can travel through the phone wires.
7. True – A commercial airplane's metal skin will conduct the current outside the airplane. The plane's fuel tanks are made to keep electrical charges from setting the fuel on fire.

8. False – Trees are tall and often struck by lightning. Only if you're in the forest and unable to get to a safe shelter can you shelter under a group of shorter trees.

9. False – A person struck by lightning will NOT be electrified. You can give them first aid as soon as possible. Lightning strike victims may need CPR and/or care for serious burns.

10. True – If you can't find shelter, make yourself as small a target as possible. Crouch down with your hands on your knees. Do NOT put your hands on the ground. Crouching in a low spot or ditch will also help.

(See endnotes. From sources 10-11)

HURRICANES

Hurricanes are the largest storms on earth. They cause billions of dollars in damage. And they are responsible for many deaths.

Depending where you live, hurricanes are called by different names. Storms that form in the Atlantic Ocean and the Eastern Pacific Ocean are called *hurricanes*. If they begin in the Western Pacific Ocean, they're *typhoons*. Those that form in the Indian Ocean are called *cyclones*. Scientists call all of these storms *tropical cyclones*.

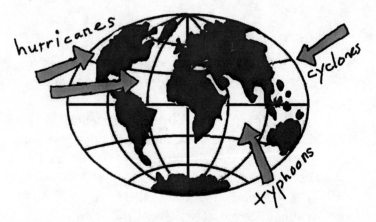

Tropical cyclones form over the warm ocean water near the equator. This super-warm, moisture-filled air rises as it heats up. The air then cools. As it goes higher into the atmosphere, the moisture in it condenses into water droplets. When the air rises, the surface air swirls in to take its place. This swirling air spins as it grows. Warm ocean water and evaporation fuel it.

The rising, moist air forms clouds and rain bands. Dry, cooler air sinks between these bands. It drops down through the center of the storm.

Tropical cyclones south of the equator spin clockwise. Those north of the equator spin counterclockwise. As the storm grows, an eye forms at its center. Inside the eye, the weather is clear and calm.

Hurricanes usually move at 10 to 15 mph toward the west. Later, they turn northwest. This gives people who live on the coast time to get ready.

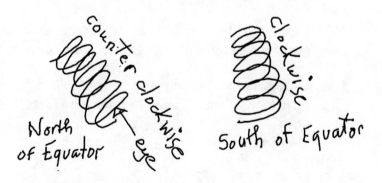

If the winds are 38 mph or less, the storm is called a *tropical depression*. If the winds reach 39 mph, it is a *tropical storm*. Then it is named. (**See "Why Hurricanes Have Names."**) When winds are 74 mph or more, it is called a *tropical cyclone* or a *Category 1 hurricane*.

(See endnotes. From sources 11-14)

Saffir-Simpson Hurricane Scale[26]

The Saffir-Simpson hurricane scale measures how destructive the hurricane is. The categories are as follows:

- **Category 1** - winds from 74 to 95 mph, causes little damage on land, and has a 4 to 5 foot storm surge

- **Category 2** – winds from 96 to 110 mph, some damage, and 6 to 8 foot storm surge

- **Category 3** – winds from 111 to 130 mph, extensive damage, and 9 to 12 foot storm surge

- **Category 4** – winds from 131 to 155 mph, extreme damage, and 13 to 18 foot storm surge

- **Category 5** – winds greater than 155 mph, catastrophic damage, and 19+ foot storm surge

Winds and rain are heavy during a hurricane. But the storm surge is the deadliest part of the storm. The low 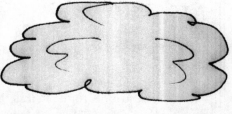 pressure inside a hurricane can suck the ocean water up several feet. As the storm nears, the high winds also push on the water. The water can rise 15 or more feet higher than the normal tides. When a hurricane reaches land, this swell of water, plus the wind-driven waves, floods low-level areas on the coast.

Most tropical cyclones weaken when they reach land. They no longer have the warm ocean water that fuels the storm. But, before the storm weakens, it can still carry high winds and heavy rainfall, and cause plenty of damage.

The Atlantic Ocean hurricane season begins on June 1 and ends on November 30. The peak season is from mid-August until late September. Most years, eleven storms are named during the season. Six usually become hurricanes. Of those, two or threes are major hurricanes (Category 3 or higher).

In 2005, there were twenty-eight named storms. Fifteen of them became hurricanes. Four were Category 5 hurricanes, setting a record. The 2005 season also caused more than 2000 deaths.

The year with the least number of tropical cyclones was 1914. Only one was recorded all season.

(See endnotes. From sources 11-14)

HIGH WAVES

HURRICANE SAFETY[16]

Hurricanes cause many dangers. They bring high winds, flooding, heavy rain, storm surges, and tornadoes. It's good to be prepared well ahead of the storm. Listen to the news on the storm's status.

Some websites post storm data and landfall predictions. Check the National Weather Service (www.weather.gov), the National Hurricane Center (www.nhc.noaa.gov), and Weather Channel (www.weather.com). If you are outside or lose power, listen for weather alerts on the NOAA Weather Radio All Hazards (NWR).

Always get ready before hurricane season starts. The National Hurricane Center (NHC) says to do the following:

- Find safe routes for evacuating
- Know where the official shelters are
- Check emergency equipment, such as flashlights, generators, cell phones, and your NOAA Weather Radio All Hazards receiver
- Buy food that will keep
- Store plenty of drinking water
- Buy wood to protect your home if you don't already have it
- Trim trees and bushes so branches don't fly into your home
- Clear clogged rain gutters and downspouts
- Decide where to move your boat
- Review your insurance policy
- Find pet-friendly hotels for when you evacuate

The NHC suggests you do the following if your home is in a Hurricane Watch area:

- Listen to radio, TV, or NOAA Weather Radio All Hazards to hear about the storm's progress
- Be sure your vehicles have gas and are drivable
- Check mobile home tie downs
- Make sure you have extra cash on hand
- Get ready to cover all windows and doors
- Check batteries in radios, phones, and flashlights
- Buy canned food, first aid supplies, drinking water, and medicine
- Bring in lightweight objects, such as garbage cans, garden tools, toys, and lawn furniture

The NHC suggests you do the following if your home is in a Hurricane Warning area:

- Listen closely to radio, TV, or NOAA Weather Radio All Hazards to find out about the storm
- Close storm shutters.
- Obey the local officials. Leave immediately if ordered!
- Find a safe place to stay or go to a shelter outside the flood zone
- DO NOT stay in a mobile or manufactured home
- Tell neighbors and a family member who lives outside the area about your plans
- Take pets with you if possible. But remember, most shelters do not allow pets unless they are needed by people with disabilities.
- Find pet-friendly hotels where you can stay

EMERGENCY SUPPLIES

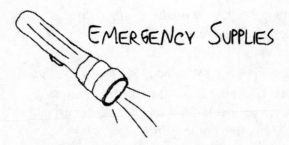

It's helpful to have emergency supplies. Pack them in a sturdy, easy-to-carry container. And put all important documents in a waterproof container.

The emergency supplies kit should have the following items:

- At least a 3-day supply of water (one gallon per person, per day)
- At least a 3-day supply of non-perishable food
- At least one change of clothing and shoes per person
- One blanket or sleeping bag per person
- First-aid kit
- Battery-powered NWR and a portable radio
- Emergency tools
- Flashlight and extra batteries
- Extra set of car keys
- Credit card and cash
- Special items for infant, elderly, or disabled family members
- Prescription and non-prescription medicines

12 CURIOUS HURRICANE FACTS

- The word *hurricane* comes from *hurucane*. This is a Taino Native American word for *evil spirit of the wind*.
- A hurricane can generate up to 20 billion tons of rain per day.
- The strongest winds of a hurricane are in the eye wall. This is the ring of thunderstorms and clouds around the hurricane's eye.
- The costliest hurricane to hit the United States was Hurricane Katrina in 2005. The storm caused $125 billion dollars in damage and killed more than 2,000 people. Hurricane Sandy in 2012 was the second costliest hurricane in the Untied States. Superstorm Sandy caused $68 billion dollars worth of damage and killed 354 people.
- The deadliest hurricane in the Atlantic Ocean was the Great Hurricane of 1780. On October 10 it hit the Caribbean, killing 25,000 people. The deadliest hurricane in the United States hit Galveston, Texas, on September 8, 1900. It had 145 mph winds. Its storm surge killed more than 8,000 people.
- Hurricanes can also produce tornadoes. But these tornadoes last only a few minutes. They are weaker than tornadoes caused by supercell thunderstorms.
- In 1967, a hurricane that hit Texas caused 140 tornadoes.

- A major hurricane gives off as much energy every second as 10 atomic bombs.

- Hurricanes move about 250 miles per day. The giant waves they create move 900 miles per day. Before weather satellites, these big waves alerted people that a hurricane was coming.
- The red spot on Jupiter is really a ginormous hurricane. It has been raging on the planet's surface for more 300 years. The size of that hurricane is larger than Earth.
- Slow-moving hurricanes can cause more damage than faster-moving storms. The slower pace allows more rain to fall, causing heavy flooding.
- Most hurricanes die before they reach land. This can happen if the storm passes over cooler water.

(See endnotes. From sources 11, 17-19)

FAMOUS ATLANTIC HURRICANES[20]

Galveston	1900
Atlantic-Gulf	1919
Miami	1926
San Felipe-Okeechobee	1928
Florida Keys Labor Day	1935
New England	1938
Great Atlantic	1944
Carol and Edna	1954
Hazel	1954
Connie and Diane	1955
Audrey	1957
Donna	1960
Camille	1969
Agnes	1972
Tropical Storm Claudette	1979
Alicia	1983
Gilbert	1988
Hugo	1989
Andrew	1992
Tropical Storm Alberto	1994
Opal	1995
Mitch	1998
Floyd	1999
Keith	2000
Tropical Storm Allison	2001
Iris	2001
Isabel	2003
Charley	2004
Frances	2004
Ivan	2004
Jeanne	2004
Dennis	2005

Katrina	2005
Rita	2005
Wilma	2005
Ike	2008
Gustav	2008
Paloma	2008
Igor	2010
Tomas	2010
Irene	2011
Sandy	2012

*This list does not include every notable storm in history.

WHY HURRICANES HAVE NAMES

By Jenna Snyder

The first person to name hurricanes was Clement Wragge, from Australia, in the late 1800s. At first he used the Greek alphabet and characters. Later he turned to naming the storms after politicians he didn't like. He could make fun of the politicians by talking about the storm using their names. Wragge's idea did not catch on, however, and not until World War II did people started naming hurricanes again.

The military and navy needed an easy way to identify hurricanes during the war. So meteorologists named them after their wives or girlfriends. In 1945, the National Weather Service used the military phonetic alphabet to label hurricanes. But they ran out of names by 1953. Once again they used women's names.

In the early 1970s, Roxcy Bolton fought for women's rights. She complained that naming hurricanes after women implied that women were disasters who destroyed everything in their paths. She suggested a similar system to Wragge's. But she wanted to use senator's names instead. Her idea was rejected. In 1979, the National Weather Service chose to alternate between men's and women's names. And it has been that way ever since.

Hurricane names are picked ahead of time for each season. The names change every six years. The list includes names from many places around the world where hurricanes have hit. Hurricanes that do a lot of damage and cost many lives have their names retired, such as Katrina, Irene, and Sandy. Another name replaces their names on the list with another name. For example, Irma replaced Irene.

A list of names for 2014 to 2018 follows:

(See endnotes. From sources 20-21)

HURRICANE NAMES
2014–2016

2014 Names	2015 Names	2016 Names
Arthur	Ana	Alex
Bertha	Bill	Bonnie
Cristobal	Claudette	Colin
Dolly	Danny	Danielle
Edouard	Erika	Earl
Fay	Fred	Fiona
Gonzalo	Grace	Gaston
Hanna	Henri	Hermine
Isaias	Ida	Ian
Josephine	Joaquin	Julia
Kyle	Kate	Karl
Laura	Larry	Lisa
Marco	Mindy	Matthew
Nana	Nicholas	Nicole
Omar	Odette	Otto
Paulette	Peter	Paula
Rene	Rose	Richard
Sally	Sam	Shary
Teddy	Teresa	Tobias
Vicky	Victor	Virginie
Wilfred	Wanda	Walter

**TROPICAL STORM LUKE HIT ASIA IN 1991.

HURRICANE NAMES
2017–2018

2017 Names	2018 Names
Arlene	Alberto
Bret	Beryl
Cindy	Chris
Don	Debby
Emily	Ernesto
Franklin	Florence
Gert	Gordon
Harvey	Helene
Irma	Isaac
Jose	Joyce
Katia	Kirk
Lee	Leslie
Maria	Michael
Nate	Nadine
Ophelia	Oscar
Philippe	Patty
Rina	Rafael
Sean	Sara
Tammy	Tony
Vince	Valerie
Whitney	William

Is YOUR name on the list?

WEATHER STATION TOOLS

3-CUP ANEMOMETER

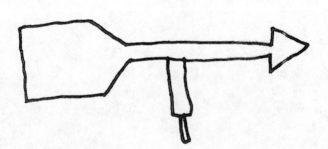

WIND DIRECTION SENSOR

RAIN GAUGE

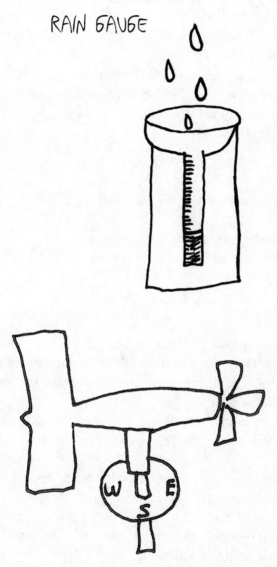

WIND SPEED AND DIRECTION SENSOR

Snowflake Experiment

Luke measured the snow with a ruler. Do you think the amount of snow that falls equals the same amount of rain? The next time it snows, try this to find out:

Supplies

- 2 clear containers of the same size
- a ruler
- tape and slips of paper for labels
- paper to record your measurements

Directions

1. Fill one container with snow, but gently place it in the container. Don't pack it down. Pull the flat edge of the ruler across the rim of the container to make the snow level with the rim.
2.. Pack snow into the other container. Pat it down so it is even on top. Use the flat edge of the ruler to level the snow.
3.. Be sure both containers are filled to the rims. Label each container so you can tell them apart after the snow turns into water.
4.. Record how deep the snow is in each container. Then guess how deep the water will be after the snow melts. Write those answers down.
5.. Let the snow melt at room temperature. This may take several hours or even overnight, depending on how warm the room is.

6.. When the snow has turned into water, measure it with the ruler.

7.. Record these measurements beside your estimates. How close were your estimates?

8.. Think about these questions: How did the amount of snow compare to the amount of water in each container? Why do you think they were different?

EXPLANATION

Snowflakes are ice crystals. Many snow crystals have six arms, or points. These points keep the snowflakes apart, leaving air space between them. That makes them take up more room. By packing down the snow, you push the snowflakes closer together. You can squeeze more snowflakes into the same sized container. The packed-down snow contains more ice crystals, so it makes more water when it melted. The more snow you pack in, the higher your water level will be.

ENDNOTES

1 National Weather Service. *Downbursts.* www.crh.noaa.gov/riw/?n=wind_safety and National Weather Service. *Microburst Wind Speeds.* http://www.erh.noaa.gov/er/cae/svrwx/washington.gif.

2 National Weather Service. *Converting Traditional Hail Size Descriptions.* http://www.spc.noaa.gov/misc/tables/hailsize.htm.

3 National Weather Service. *Record Setting Hail Event in Vivian, South Dakota on July 23, 2010.* http://www.crh.noaa.gov/abr/?n=stormdamagetemplate.

4 National Weather Service. *What about Hail.* http://www.erh.noaa.gov/box/hail.html.

5 Weather Underground, Inc. *Severe Storms and Supercells.* http://www.wunderground.com/resources/severe/severe_storms.asp.

6 National Weather Service. *Tornado FAQ.* http://www.spc.noaa.gov/faq/tornado/index.html.

7 Erdman, Jonathan. *Tornado Perspective: Deaths, Width, Path Lengths.* The Weather Channel. April 26, 2010. http://www.weather.com/outlook/weather-news/news/articles/0426-tornado-deaths-stats_2010-04-26?page=2.

8 Johnstown Flood Museum. *History of the Johnstown Flood.* http://www.jaha.org/FloodMuseum/history.html.

9 Roach, John. *Key to Lightning Deaths: Location, Location, Location.* National Geographic News. June 22, 2004. http://news.nationalgeographic.com/news/2003/05/0522_030522_lightning.html

10 National Weather Service. *Lightning Safety.* http://www.lightningsafety.noaa.gov/index.htm.

11 Lyons, Walter A. *The Handy Weather Answer Book.* Detroit, MI: Visible Ink Press, 1997.

12 NASA. *How Do Hurricanes Form?* http://spaceplace.nasa.gov/hurricanes/

13 National Weather Service. Tropical Cyclone Climatology. http://www.nhc.noaa.gov/climo/#ncy

14 National Weather Service. *National Hurricane Center.* http://www.nhc.noaa.gov/.

15 Janiskee, Bob. *Shenandoah National Park Ranger Roy Sullivan Set the World Record for Being Hit by Lightning.* National Parks Traveler. August 1, 2008. http://www.nationalparkstraveler.com/2008/08/shenandoah-national-park-ranger-roy-sullivan-set-world-record-being-hit-lightning.

16 National Weather Service. *Hurricane Preparedness Week.* http://www.nhc.noaa.gov/prepare/.

17 National Weather Service. *Most Extreme Tropical Cyclones.* http://www.nhc.noaa.gov/dcmi.shtml.

18 Hurricane Facts. *Interesting Hurricane Facts.* http://www.hurricane-facts.com/Interesting-Hurricane-Facts.php.

19 Hurricane Facts. *More Hurricane Facts.* http://www.hurricane-facts.com/More-Hurricane-Facts.php.

20 National Weather Service. *Hurricanes in History.* http://www.nhc.noaa.gov/outreach/history/.

21 Cohen, Jennie. *Why Do Hurricanes Have Names?* History in the Headlines. August 25, 2011. http://www.history.com/news/why-do-hurricanes-have-names.

22 National Weather Service. *Tropical Cyclone Names.* http://www.nhc.noaa.gov/aboutnames.shtml.

23 National Weather Service. *Electrication.* http://www.lightningsafety.noaa.gov/science/science_electrication.htm.

24 National Weather Service. *Thunder.* http://www.lightningsafety.noaa.gov/science/science_thunder.htm.

25 National Weather Service. *Summary of Historic Floods and Flash Floods.* http://www.crh.noaa.gov/unr/?n=history.

26 National Weather Service. *Saffir-Simpson Hurricane Wind Scale.* http://www.nhc.noaa.gov/aboutsshws.php.

HURRICANE SYMBOL FOR WEATHER MAPS

If you enjoyed *Storm Watcher*, you might enjoy these Leap Books...

Island Sting

by Bonnie J. Doerr

Intrepid teens track down the poacher of the endangered Key deer. But will they survive when the killer turns from stalking deer to hunting humans?

Stakeout

by Bonnie J. Doerr

Involved in a new undercover sting, the Keys teens plan to save a different endangered species. This time they try to capture the criminals who are robbing sea turtle nests. Danger, intrigue, and mystery await them at every turn.

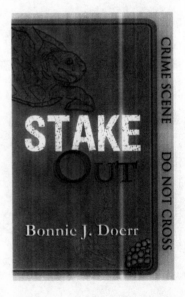

Case of the Invisible Witch

by Patrice Lyle

Spells and Spies is an under-cover PI service at Poison Ivy Charm School, a prep school for witches and warlocks. The private eyes have 72 hours to discover the culprit who turned a classmate invisible. If they don't, she'll disappear forever .

Chase
by
Sydney Scrogham

In an epic battle of good and evil, Chase must gather his forces to defeat the cruel Snyx before it wipes out the land of miniature winged horses and destroys a human Chase loves.

Thank you for purchasing this Leap Books publication. For other exciting teen novels, please visit our online bookstore at www.leapbks.net.

For questions or more information contact us at leapbks@gmail.com

Leap Books
www.leapbks.net

CPSIA information can be obtained at www.ICGtesting.com
Printed in the USA
LVOW11s2009161113

361592LV00008B/1096/P